FISTS OF LOVE

KAMI

Paroxysm Press
PO Box 3107
Rundle Mall
Adelaide
5000
[Australia]

http://paroxysmpress.com
paroxysm@paroxysmpress.com
facebook.com/paroxysmpress
instagram.com/paroxysmpress

Fists Of Love
Kami
ISBN 978-1-876502-28-7

Cover art & design: Meg Wright (Red Wallflower Photography)
facebook.com/redwallflower
instagram.com/red.wallflower

Dedicated to Michael Sharp (Sharpy)

16/5/64 – 21/2/21

The Original Gangster

Time Stands Still

"No one's gonna ever cause you any pain, no one's gonna hurt you no more/ To get to you, my honey, they'll have to break down my door"

© Chris D 1984 Shakeytown Music

Prologue

The rain was cold on his back. Not a heavy downpour, just a drizzle, cold and tiptoeing across his spine, his bare arse, his legs. It didn't stop them though. It was Christmas morning, 3.45am, nine months and sixteen days since their son had died, six months exactly since they had separated and now they were naked on her back lawn, fucking. Not a word passed between them just grunts, moans, air pushing in and out from mouth and groin. He felt the familiar tingling, felt his toes starting to curl as they always did and he came. He was always in two minds after orgasm; the feeling was so good, so intense but then there was always the feeling of disappointment that the act was over, a sense of loss, finality. She heard his toes crack, felt the final thrust as he let go and the movement stopped. She clutched his back holding him inside her, once again wishing he could have held on just a little longer. Slowly he rolled off of her and lay sweating on the lawn, light rain now sprinkling his chest. He peeled the condom off his now shrinking dick and flung it towards the cat who was watching from the shelter of the tank stand. She hadn't moved, just lay there breathing heavily, eyes closed. Raising himself on one elbow he looked at her.

He could see drips of rain sitting, resting on her pubis and breasts. Her stomach was damp with rain, sweat and saliva. All was quiet now. As if conscious of his steady gaze, she turned towards him and opened her eyes. There was nothing there. She said two words, "Go home." then closed her eyes and turned away.

He stood on the back verandah, pulling his jeans on, watching her. She was pure white against the black of night and he remembered a line from a poem he'd read once:

> *When he made you*
> *He came all over his blessed universe*

She hadn't moved. As he turned to leave she rolled over and watched him. She didn't get up until she heard his car starting, the stereo too loud for this hour of the morning. Only then did she gather up the energy to rise and collect her clothes from the lawn. She went inside and ran a hot shower. Outside the cat sniffed around the discarded condom, tapped it lightly with both front paws and then turned and walked away.

One

Cindy put the suitcase by the door next to her backpack and turned to take one last look at her room. Not that there was much to see. She'd already stripped the bed, leaving the sheets on the floor, the pillow now sitting on the naked mattress. A towel hung on the end of the bed still damp. On the wall were three posters, none of them hers. They'd been left there by previous tenants, the boy with leukemia left the Guns'n'Roses print when he went home after his last marrow transplant, the girl who died from the brain tumour had put up the kittens. Cindy hadn't had the heart to take them down though she had at first hated the smiling cats, the message of hope coming from the voice balloon above their heads. But she had come to the realisation that she always looked at them as soon as she walked into the room, especially after another visit to the doctor or after getting test results. Over the last seven months she had looked at those smiling cats a lot. Owen House had been her home since she'd left hospital. It was a halfway house where she could rebuild her strength as she underwent ongoing treatment, chemotherapy, listened to the vague promises of recovery. Soon though she had grown tired, the promises rang false in her ears and she realised she no longer had the strength, the will power to continue the fight. It had surprised her. She'd always considered herself a fighter; feisty, lively, born to cause trouble and strike back, all the classic bad girl clichés but this time the fight had been taken out of her. She'd had enough of it all and the realist in her had taken over. Life wasn't worth the struggle, the pain if the treatment to prolong it always left her weak, nauseous and flat on her back with just the smiling felines and Axl Rose to watch over her. It was time to go home and there was only one man who would take her, who could take her.

Jason sat in the car, AC/DC on the tape deck, tapping the steering wheel in time to the beat. A 1967 HR Holden, stick-shift '3 on a tree', faded green exterior, faded red interior. Jason had borrowed it from his stepfather Dave.

It was the car that Dave had taught him to drive in back when he was 16, the car they had worked on together, a car he knew almost intimately. The HR had been a bonding between Jason and Dave. Dave had come along when Jason was 12 going on 13 and it had taken two or three years for Jason to accept Dave as his mother's husband, as his stepfather. The car was the turning point for both of them. They worked on it together, repairing, cleaning, patching up the rust, wiring up the tape deck and speakers. And then Dave taught Jason how to drive in it. Dave had kept the car all these years because it reminded him of that time, of the moment when Jason had first called him 'dad'. He didn't drive it much anymore but he refused to part with it. As he'd handed the keys over to his stepson this morning he'd felt something like pride welling inside of him. Jason had turned out okay he thought and just maybe he'd had a hand in that. Even though Jason was an adult now, Dave still saw that skinny kid hiding behind his mother that first morning that Dave had stood in the kitchen being introduced to the boys. He still saw that boy who wasn't sure about letting another father figure into his life, who was scared of losing another dad. Dave had hung in there though and this car was part of that, this faded green Holden was in essence, their bond, the link that held these two men together, that had made them both feel like they were finally a family. They both stood silently looking the car over, Jason toying with the keys in his hand, Dave running a finger over the roof, feeling the bubbling rust coming up in spots. "Must fix that up when he comes back," he thought to himself before turning to his stepson.

They shook hands. "Have a good trip son."

Jason nodded, climbed in and started the car. It felt good to hear the old motor click over, hear that muffled roar as he gassed it, three pumps to get the juices flowing just like they used to do when he was first learning.

Now as Jason sat in the cool morning sunshine, Bon Scott telling him "The girl's got rhythm…" he wondered whether or not he should have borrowed the new car instead. He had a long way to drive after all and the old HR wasn't even air-conditioned.

"What the hell am I doing?" he said out loud to himself, "I'm too old for a road trip anyway. That's the sort of shit you do when you're 21 not 36."

Then Cindy came out of the house, pausing for one last look before pulling the door shut behind her. She walked purposefully across the lawn, carrying her suitcase and backpack, closed the gate as she stepped out onto the sidewalk and stood by the car. She turned and looked at the house. She wasn't coming back, she knew that and for a moment she felt a flicker of something, grief, loss… she wasn't sure. She shook her head, turned back to the car and waited.

Jason realised that she was waiting for him to take her bags and put them in the boot. He clambered out of the car, snagging himself on the seatbelt.

"You've got to unclip yourself first," sniggered Cindy.

He grunted, unclipped the seatbelt, thankful they'd never got around to putting in the retractable type and shrugged it off. "Sorry, I was miles away."

He fumbled with his keys, trying to remember which one opened the boot.

"Try the ignition key," said Cindy.

Jason shook his head. "No, we had to change the lock a few years back. The old one got a key jammed in it."

"How'd you manage that?"

He looked at her. "Who said it was me?"

He found the key, opened the boot.

"Well… was it?"

He pushed his suitcase back and squeezed her two in, next to the water bottle and the spare tire. "Yeah, it was. I was drunk and I broke the key off."

He shrugged. "It was the wrong key."

Cindy smiled. "And Dave let you borrow the car?"

"Hey, I'm his favourite stepson, what can I say?"

He got back in the car and fiddled with the keys again. Cindy climbed in the passenger side.

"Ready to roll?" Jason asked.

She nodded. "Ready," she said softly.

He started the car. They were on the road.

The car was idling at the lights still waiting for the red man to stop flashing, still waiting for the old biddy to shakily make her way across the pedestrian crossing when Cindy turned to Jason. "Can we go to the cemetery first?" she asked quietly, "I'd like to say goodbye to Hank."

"I guess so," he mumbled then putting the car in the wrong gear, kangaroo hopped across the intersection. Cursing he pulled the gear stick down, "Shit, got to get used to the stick shift again."

Cindy said nothing.

He parked the HR under some pine trees and they got out. The air was fresh, clean, and Jason could smell the pine needles underfoot, it reminded him of home. Then he saw the crumbling marble crosses in the old section of the cemetery and remembered why he was here. He hadn't been back to this place in three years, since Hank's funeral, since the day he'd dropped the first sprinkle of dirt on his son's coffin and had to hold his mum up as she almost fainted. He'd never had the courage to come back, tried to hide his grief in beer and blondes. No wonder Cindy had hated him so much after Hank's death. He took a deep breath and turned a full circle, taking in the trees, the blue sky and the graves. He didn't want to be here.

Cindy was standing at the gate. "You coming?"

He nodded. "Yeah, just getting my bearings."

They walked slowly towards Hank's grave. Jason had to follow Cindy; he couldn't remember where his son's final resting place was. Mentally he was punching himself around the head for being so selfish, so stupid, so much a coward. Cindy didn't hesitate, knowing exactly where to walk; it was a path she had walked many times. There were fresh flowers on the grave.

Cindy looked at Jason, "You?"

He shook his head, almost ashamed. "Maybe Dave? I don't know."

She bent down, sniffed the flowers, plucked the dead leaves off and then picking the vase up, left Jason standing at the gravesite while she went to get fresh water.

Jason looked at the plaque. *Hank Myers 16/1/1999 – 9/3/2003 Loving son of Jason & Cindy Rest In Peace.* There was a photo in the corner, Hank's fourth birthday, his last, his face beaming, full of joy, full of life. Jason felt the tear running down his cheek. He wiped it away.

"You're weak," he said to himself, "you left her alone, you should have been there for her. This is all your fault."

He flinched as Cindy put her hand on his shoulder. "You okay?"

"Huh… sure, sure. I… I haven't been here for a while, it just caught me a bit…"

She knelt, put the vase back down carefully, fiddled with the flowers again. "I know. I still have trouble with it. Do you think it ever gets any easier?"

Jason shrugged. "I don't know. I still think about my cousin Michael and he died ten, fifteen years ago. I don't think about him all the time but he's still in here," he tapped his head, "maybe we never forget, I think we just try not to remember so much, if that makes sense."

Cindy smiled. "No, not really." She stood up. "I don't think I could ever not remember Hank."

Jason blushed, feeling out of place here amongst green lawns and quiet breeze, the smell of pine needles still in the air, while his son lay dead at his feet. "I guess I mean… well, we don't forget them but we have to go on, we can't just stop. So, they're there in the back of our heads, in our memories but we don't face them daily, don't constantly think about them."

Cindy slipped her hand into his. "I think I know what you're saying even though you say it so poorly."

"Yeah, for a man who talks so much I really have nothing to say."

"Good thing you were good in bed."

They both went quiet. It didn't seem right to be smiling and joking right now, right here but it felt better than being miserable.

Jason broke the silence. "I miss the little bugger so much. There are days when I wake up and half expect him to come bounding in and jump on the bed to tell me what's happened on Blues Clues or what he wants for breakfast."

"And then you realise that you're alone?"

He looked at her. "Yeah," he said almost whispering, "then I realise that I'm alone."

He could feel her hand squeezing his. "I don't want to be alone anymore Jason."

"Neither do I Cindy, neither do I."

Cindy Voorhees, third from the front, look of arrogance on her face, black choker around her neck, eyes dark, black hair pulled back, bruise barely visible on her right cheek…

She looked again at the photo. It was her Year 10 class shot, three months before she was kicked out for smoking dope in the toilets. She stared at the girl; it didn't seem that it was her at all, only the arrogant look seemed familiar. Was she really like that? Was that truly her, this self-righteous little bitch in the photo, trying so hard to look tough, like nothing mattered? Did this girl know that this was her last school photo? That she would never again be posing like this, with school friends, in a classroom situation? Could this girl have known what she was doing that day she lit up in the toilets, passing a pipe of bad homegrown and leaf around just as the headmistress walked in?

She slid the photo across the table to Jason. "Here, have a laugh." Jason put his burger down and picked up the photograph. "Careful," she said, "don't get it greasy."

Gingerly he kept his fingers on the edges. "Wow, you were a tough little bitch, weren't you?"

She couldn't tell if he was mocking her or not.

"It was a tough class." She gestured. "See the boy standing behind me? Johnny Casanova…"

He looked at the boy – slicked back hair, brown almond eyes, tanned – he hated him on the spot.

"Johnny was already a dad when that photo was taken. And the girl next to me… Sally…" She shrugged. "Sally topped herself in Year 12. The exams got to her."

Jason put the photo back down. "Do you see any of these kids anymore?"

"Not really. That was a long time ago. Once I left school I lost touch with most of them." She slipped the photo back into its envelope. "And then Mum and Dad moving us to Queensland..."

She stopped, not wanting to tell him why they moved, not really wanting to acknowledge it herself. They had moved to try to give Cindy another chance, to try to get her back into school, to give her another shot at getting things right. It hadn't worked.

Jason offered her some fries. "Want some?"

"No, that's okay. They taste funny. The chemo I guess, things taste different now."

He looked at his watch. "Do you want to get going then? I'd like to get to Woodfern before it gets too late."

"Or before the pub shuts," she smiled.

"That, too."

She picked up her bag, the envelope and then waited as Jason finished off his Coke.

"Okay, I'm ready."

She looked at her reflection in the door as he opened it for her. Her hair was short, lax and dull, the eyes still sparkled but she could see the dimness coming, she fancied, could see the flame being extinguished. And her body, she looked like Celine Dion on a crash diet – it scared her. She'd avoided mirrors the past few weeks, not wanting to see what she'd become, what had disappeared. She felt weakened by her image, her lack of physical substance, of form.

Jason took her by the arm. "You okay?"

She tried to smile. "Yeah, just getting used to my supermodel looks."

"Hey, they got me back," he grinned.

"Great. Just what I needed, a sympathy fuck."

"I get a fuck, too? You didn't tell me that."

She laughed. It felt good. He led her out the door.

"Come on, let's get to Mum's. I hope she's given us the double bed. After all, I'm on a promise now."

They got to Woodfern just on dark. Jason saw the familiar sign – 'BP Service Station 2KM' – bullet holes through the B, empty beer cans scattered around, and he knew he was home. He wound down the window and took a deep breath, the smell of pine needles and roadkill wafted in. Yeah he was home. His first twenty one years had been spent in this country alcove. He'd had his first cigarette behind Woodfern High School's change rooms; bought his first bottle of Brandivino at 15 at the Woodfern Bottle shop; got his first stinky finger; lost a father, gained a stepfather, got engaged, married and divorced in this town, before leaving for the big smoke.

Now he was passing through on another journey, on the road and taking Cindy home to die. He looked across at her asleep on the passenger side. She was so frail looking now, so tiny. The disease had wasted her body away, piece by piece but still she clung on, her spirit refusing to fade. He was amazed at how tough she was, how resilient, he doubted whether he could show that much courage, that much fight if it was he who had been diagnosed.

He remembered the night she broke the news to him. He hadn't seen her for a couple of months, not since she'd come out of hospital the second time. He'd tried to support her but work and stupidity and the tension between them had kept him away. Then she rang him and asked him around for tea. Over spaghetti she finally told him.

"It's over," she said casually as she sprinkled parmesan cheese on her spaghetti.

He pushed the pasta around on his plate. "What does that mean?" he asked, not really wanting the answer.

She looked at her food, not really hungry at all, the smell of the cheese making her nauseous. She pushed her plate away.

"It means I've had enough, Jase. I'm not letting them cut me up any more." She ran her fingers across her scalp, through the thinning hair struggling to regrow. "They can't save me now and I'm tired. Tired of fighting it, tired of being their guinea pig, tired of life…"

He put down his fork, reached across the table and took her hand in his. "You have to fight it, Cindy. What am I supposed to do without you? Who's going to call me on the phone in the middle of the night and tell me what a bastard I am? Who's going to set fire to my mailbox or threaten to beat up my girlfriends at the pub? You can't leave me."

She smiled. "I already left you remember? After the blonde, that barmaid… what was her name? Linda?"

"Okay, okay. And her name was Lindsay. That's not the point. We still have a history, we still have the memories." He could feel the tears welling up in his eyes.

Absent-mindedly he rubbed the tattoo on his arm, the tattoo of Hank, the tattoo he'd had done the day of the funeral. Lightly, Cindy ran her fingers over his other bicep. "Put me on the other arm," she said quietly. He'd stayed the night, just holding her while she cried and she told him she wanted to go home to die. She wanted to be with her mother and he'd agreed to take her, to drive her back to Queensland.

Now, as he turned into Woodfern's main street, their first night into the journey, Cindy already asleep and looking exhausted, drawn, so 'old china' frail, he wondered if she would survive the trip, if she would even make it home.

Two

His mum was waiting when they pulled into the drive. He thought she might have put on some weight but he wasn't going to tell her that. Her hair was in a tight bun, a curl loose over one ear. The dressing gown pulled tightly around her waist didn't help hide the extra weight. She stepped off the porch smiling as they climbed out of the car.

"Hello darling," she said to Cindy. She took her by the arm and led her towards the house. Jason stood on the lawn.

"Hey! Remember me, your son? The good-looking one?"

The front door swung open. "Don't be silly, Jason. Get your things and come inside. The poor girl needs some nourishment. You, however, need to lose some weight." The front door swung shut.

"Missed you too, Mum," he muttered as he collected their bags from the boot.

Inside, the house was cluttered with knick-knacks and stuffed toys. There were newspapers piled up next to her armchair, catalogues strewn across the coffee table, dishes sat on the sink and coffee-stained cups seemed to turn up everywhere he looked. It had been like this since Dave had gone to the city on a work transfer. His mum had refused to move. She stayed home, making Dave travel back and forth every couple of weekends to see her. Dave joked that it was like courting her again but the boys didn't see the joke.

"So, you're still single then?" he asked as he shooed the cat off a chair. She nodded.

"Yes, dear. You know that. You are driving David's car after all."

He sighed. "Why don't you just move up to town, Mum? I'm too old to have separated parents."

"What would I do in the city? I've told your brother Bradley and I'm telling you, my friends are here. My reading group, my flower arranging class, the CWA…I couldn't leave all that."

Cindy stood behind her, smiling. "You tell him, Sylvie, we don't need men."

Jason threw the car keys to her. "Fine then, girl, you drive and I'll sleep all the way. It's only a couple of thousand clicks after all."

His mother gave him the look she used to save for when he brought his report cards home.

"Stop being silly, Jason. Now I've got some soup on the stove and there's fresh bread on the table. Help yourself while I get your rooms ready."

"Rooms?"

"Oh yes. She's much too ill to have you lumbering in drunk…" Sylvie stopped, turned to Cindy. "I'm sorry dear, I didn't mean to…" Cindy waved it off.

"No, you're right, Sylvie. I'm too ill to have that boofhead falling on top of me drunk. Look what happened last time."

Sylvie dabbed at her eyes. "I do miss him. He was such a lovely little boy. It just doesn't seem fair, first little Hank and now you. I wonder what I've done sometimes to deserve all this."

Cindy bit her tongue.

"What I want to know is what I've done to deserve this? You know I hate beef and vegetable soup, Mum," said Jason from the kitchen.

His mother glared. "You are so much like your father. I don't know what I saw in him."

Cindy smiled to herself. She knew he was trying to distract Sylvie before she had them all wallowing in self-pity and prayer meetings.

"Anyway," continued Jason, "who said I'd be going down to the pub?"

Both women just looked at him. He put his hands up. "Okay, stupid question."

The front bar at the Royal hadn't changed. Well, except for the five colour screens above the tote boards that constantly showed horse races, results and tote odds from across the country. But it still had the Winfield Red clock over the bar and it was still five minutes slow. The old wooden-door coolers that never really chilled the beer properly were still there, as was the pool table that rolled to the left. In the fireplace smoldered two damp, slightly green chunks of red gum, old Fred was still at the end of the bar nursing a butcher of porter gaff and Johnno the barman still had a bad haircut and 70s porno moustache.

"Jason Myers, as I live and breathe. What are you doing in town?"

Jason pulled up a stool. "Just passing through, Johnno. Any of the boys out tonight?"

Johnno slid a coaster over and started pouring a beer. "Not here. Eightball's out at Mt Barren tonight. They won't be back till maybe 11, if they win that is." He put Jason's beer on the coaster. "And they won't. They're bloody hopeless. Can't even beat the sheilas' team."

"Nothing's changed then?"

"Not a bloody thing, mate, not a bloody thing." Jason had two beers and left. If the team had won he wouldn't have got home in time to watch Cindy O.D.

Cindy woke feeling groggy and lost. The room smelt clean, like disinfectant and lemons. There was a curtain pulled around the bed. She stared at the light blue ceiling. She was in hospital again.

What the hell had happened? The last thing she remembered was Jason walking into her bedroom as she was shooting up.

"What the fuck are you doing?"

"Isn't it obvious?" Then black.

She sensed someone to her right and slowly turned her head. Jason and Sylvie sat there. Sylvie looked worried, Jason looked pissed off.

"You okay, dearie?" asked Sylvie gently. "You gave us quite a scare." Cindy nodded. Sylvie took her hand. "You'll be okay now. They have very good doctors in Woodfern. You'll be up in no time."

Jason said nothing, just stared at her. Cindy sat up gingerly and reached for the water jug. She felt even weaker than normal, tired, washed out and slow…a feeling of not quite connecting, of moments passed before you realise.

It was like being back in hospital for the operations again, that grogginess, that sense of displacement, of days gone never to return. She sipped the water carefully, taking her time and marveling at the taste. She'd never felt so parched before, never felt so thirsty.

Sylvie was still talking, words drifting in and out, crossing each other out in the air, overriding and repeating.

"Quite a scare…not that I was really worried…but Jason was quite shaken, weren't you, dear? Oh yes, quite a scare… we should let you rest… is there anything you need…?"

Jason still said nothing. Cindy shook her head and lay back down.

Sylvie stood and patted her on the forehead. "We'll come back this afternoon. You rest now, dear."

Jason took her hand, squeezed but she could see in his eyes he was angry. He left the room without saying a word.

Sergeant Joseph Forrest had been at Woodfern forever it seemed. Jason remembered being busted by him maybe 20 years ago now for underage drinking, his torch shining obtrusively in the back of someone's car to find Jason and Cheryl Barker lip-locked, half dressed and totally drunk. He'd got away with a warning and blue balls that night. He didn't think he'd be so lucky this time.

On the table in front of Jason lay the syringe, bagged and labeled. Forrest sat on the other side of the table.

"So, Jason, haven't seen you for a long while. Your mother tells me you live in the big smoke now." He paused, smiled. "Own a record shop, don't you?"

Jason shook his head. "Not anymore."

Forrest glanced at the syringe. "Money trouble?"

"What? No, nothing like that." He felt insulted. "It just got away from me."

He thought back to the shop, The Vinyl Jungle. All he'd ever wanted was to run a record shop. It had been a continuing teenage fantasy, along with

Cheryl Barker. But after the accident, after burying Hank, he'd found it impossible to stay focused, to care. He was always late, some days not even bothering to open, and when he did open there was no new stock, no help for the customers, just hangovers and surly abuse. Bills didn't get paid, the stock got lower and he ran out of dreams.

"I just wasn't cut out to be a businessman I guess…easier to be paid by someone else."

Forrest nodded. "Yes, not all of us are suited to our own businesses." He picked up the syringe. "Now…would you like to tell me about this?"

"What's to tell? It's not mine."

Forrest stood up. "Did I say it was?" He patted his pockets. "You don't have a cigarette do you? I'm trying to give up."

Jason smiled. "Sorry, don't smoke."

The syringe was placed back on the table. Jason could see initials carved into the tabletop, next to them: 'I was framed.'

"I know this doesn't belong to you, Jason, but you must surely have known your wife was using it."

"She's not my wife."

Forrest frowned. "Don't split hairs. Your partner, wife, girlfriend is in hospital recovering from a heroin overdose. You knew she was an addict."

Jason looked up at the big man. There were deep lines across his forehead, grey around the thinning edges of hair, bags under the eyes – he no longer looked intimidating, just another old man.

"No, I didn't. We hadn't seen much of each other lately, not until she got sick anyway."

Forrest sat back down, crossed his arms. "Yes, your mother mentioned that. How long?" The question hung between them. Jason looked at the initials, the syringe, the reflection of light bouncing off the plastic bag wrapped around it.

"Not long," he finally said quietly, "not long at all."

They both sat in silence with only the hum of the fluoro above and the faint drone of traffic outside to remind them that they weren't the only ones alive right now. Jason just wanted to stop everything, wrap himself in a blanket and block it all out – the light, the sounds, the knowledge – he wanted none of it. Forrest stood up, pocketing the syringe.

"Well, I've got a lot of paperwork to do before I process this. It will probably be tomorrow morning before I can even serve your friend with a summons," he paused, looked at Jason, "If she's still here…"

He reached over the table, patted Jason's shoulder. "Be careful. It's a big world out there and you're still that kid I busted with his tongue down Cheryl Barker's throat," he laughed. "Now she's got three kids and an arse bigger than mine. You just be careful."

He walked out leaving Jason alone with the initials, the light and a thirst.

Cindy was watching TV when he walked in. "Hi, how are you?"

He mumbled something then reaching for the remote, flicked off the TV. "I said it's time to go."

"What? Why?" But she knew. He started packing her clothes into the overnight bag Sylvie had supplied.

"Forrest has given you a break." He looked at her. "You're lucky. Right now the only break I'd offer you is your neck."

Cindy recoiled. She'd never seen him like this before.

"I'm sorry, Jason. I didn't think you'd take it like this."

He stopped, dropped the bag on the floor.

"Like what? What did you expect? Flowers? After all, you were only shooting up in my mum's spare room."

"Please don't shout. I don't think everyone else needs to know."

He picked up the bag, threw it on the chair.

"Oh, they know already. Don't worry, in a town this size, they know." He threw her jeans on the bed. "Get dressed, we've got some traveling to do."

They were parked in a truck stop outside Mildura. It had been a long and silent drive until finally Jason had pulled over to pour himself a coffee from the thermos that had rattled around in the back for the whole journey.

"So, where is it?"

She thought about lying to him but felt too tired to fight. Picking up the thermos, she pulled off a lid at the bottom.

"In the bottom here." Something dropped out. "It's a space to keep your sweetener."

He looked at the small bag of powder sitting so unobtrusively in her lap.

How much would that be worth, he wondered. "So, how long you been using?"

"I'm not an addict, Jason. It's for the pain." She picked up the sachet. "In hospital they gave me morphine. It was good for the pain, for keeping it all away. I missed it when I got out." She shook the sachet. "This helps."

Jason reached over, taking it from her hand before she could stop him. "I should just throw this shit out the window."

"I'd just get more," she said defiantly. It was the strongest he'd heard her sound for weeks.

"Yeah, you probably would." He threw it back at her. "Hide it and go easy, I don't need another O.D."

She took it.

"I'm sorry about that. It wasn't supposed to happen, this stuff is just stronger than I'm used to." She put the lid back on the thermos. "I'll be more careful now I know."

"You do that." He tipped the rest of the coffee out of the window. "Didn't you at least pack some sugar?"

"There wasn't enough room, sorry."

He started the car.

"You are going to kill me, you know that?"

Cindy smiled. "Do you think I have enough time?"

Three

They were back on the highway, a new moon struggling to add any light to the evening sky when Cindy asked, "So how do you know Forrest anyway?"

Jason grinned, turned to her. "I was a Demented Jellybean."

"A what?"

"A Demented Jellybean. It was a street gang in Woodfern."

She laughed. "Woodfern had a street gang?"

He reached across, punching her arm in mock umbrage. "Two in fact, Miss Smarty-pants, The Cobras and The Jellybeans."

"And you were a Jellybean?"

"Founding member," he said proudly, "me, Johnno and Pete the Stud."

"Pete the Stud?" She studied his face, trying to work out if he was serious or not.

He flicked on the headlights, the highway stretching ahead barely illuminated in the new moon. Trucks came past, their lights filling the car temporarily, giving Cindy a strange glow. Jason shivered as he noticed how drawn and pale she seemed under those accusing headlights. Cindy seemed not to notice.

"Yeah, Pete the Stud. So named because he got even less action than me."

She smirked, "Is that possible? I thought you told me you were hopeless with the girls."

"Just the one."

He thought back to the night the Jellybeans were founded. Cheryl Barker had laughed at him over the phone when he'd asked her out so he'd consoled himself with a flagon of cheap wine and the company of Johnno and Pete. They'd been sitting in the council chambers' car park when the Cobras slinked past. There were eight of them, 14 years and younger and all dressed in black.

"What the fuck is that?" he asked Johnno.

"That's the Cobras." He took a slug of the flagon. "Woodfern's got a street gang now."

"Since when?"

"Since they showed *The Warriors* at the drive-in," laughed Pete.

Jason was quite indignant. "What gives those little shits the right to roam the streets? These are our streets, we spend the most time on them."

"Only because our parents won't let you in our houses, Myers," countered Johnno.

"That's a technicality. If Woodfern is going to have a street gang, then it should be us." Jason took another swig on the flagon. Surely being in a street gang would impress Cheryl Barker.

"So what do we call ourselves?" asked Johnno from the back seat, where he always seemed to end up, even in his own car.

Jason looked at Pete's green T-shirt, Johnno's light blue sweatshirt and down at his own red checked flanny.

"Demented Jellybeans," he proclaimed and the boys toasted until Pete threw up all over the driver's side door.

Jason's reminiscing intrigued Cindy, he hadn't mentioned this story before. "So, you were in a gang, albeit with the stupidest name this side of the Rabbitohs. Did you ever rumble?"

"Not really. A few of us would stand in the car park waving hockey sticks and empty bottles at the Cobras as they walked past…"

"What did they do?"

"They'd run. After all they were maybe 13, 14. We were 16, 17, Johnno had just turned 18…of course they ran."

He pulled the tape out of the tape player, threw it over the back seat. "Have a look in the glove box, there should be a tape labeled 'Music For Demented Jellybeans'. It was our soundtrack."

Cindy found the tape and put it on. Nostalgia washed over him. "This was our theme song," he said as Skyhooks' *This Town Is Boring* came on. "This one and *Why Doncha All Get Fucked*."

She smirked. "Real pick-up songs then?"

"Yeah, I gotta admit it was very hard to pick up with Pete in the back singing *Why Doncha All Get Fucked* at the top of his lungs." He turned the tape down. "Not that we ever picked up anyway."

"I find that hard to believe," she said only half-joking.

He shrugged. "I wasn't always this cool, you know. Hard to believe but I was once a dork."

"It's not that hard actually." She reached over and put her hand on his leg. "Tell me more about Woodfern, about you."

He looked at her in the dim glow of the car's dash-lights. She was smiling but she still looked so tired. "What do you want to know?"

"Well…you said Forrest knew you."

"He knew everyone, he's an old-fashioned cop, that's his job." He turned on the heater.

"He was always around, busting us for drinking or speeding. Once he caught Pete pissing in the main street."

"And what happened?"

"Case was dropped for lack of evidence," laughed Jason.

Cindy grinned. "You've been saving that line for a long time."

Jason put one hand on hers. She was cold. He reached over and turned the heater up.

"So that's it? Forrest knew you because you were the local larrikins?"

Jason hesitated. "There was a fight once…we got involved."

Cindy frowned. "I thought you said you didn't fight?"

"We didn't start it, we just arrived in the middle of it." He wondered just how much he should tell her. "Some kids from Mt Barren came to town to fight the Cobras. They kicked their arses."

"Who, the Cobras?" She wasn't following what he was saying and she had an idea he was holding back on something, too. He wasn't as eager to talk now.

Jason shook his head. "Nah, the Cobras got flogged. It wasn't a fair fight. Those kids were 14, the guys from Mt Barren were maybe 20, 21…" He paused, took a deep breath. "So we took them on."

"And?"

"And we were getting our arses flogged, too."

"What happened?"

This is the moment, he thought, this is where you drown or swim.

"Johnno pulled a .22 from the boot. It was his brother's. We won."

Cindy was stunned. "You used a gun?"

"No, Johnno did." He already regretted telling her. "It wasn't loaded but they didn't know that. That was when Forrest got involved."

He looked at her; her face was a mask. The gun story wasn't something anyone talked about anymore. Everyone involved tried to forget it or ignore it. The gun was loaded but only Johnno and Jason knew that, even Pete thought it was empty. Jason still remembered the sight of Johnno standing on the bonnet of Mark Handley's car waving the gun and telling them all to get back to Mt Barren before he blew their fucking heads off.

The Cobras may have been a bunch of punk kids but they didn't deserve the flogging they were getting that night. Deep down the boys admired the little fuckers' attitude, the stance they had taken in a town as insular as Woodfern. They were brave kids, if a little dumb. And Handley and his mates shouldn't have done what they'd done. It was an unfair fight, Johnno just evened it up. At least that was what they kept telling each other afterwards.

Jason was watching Cindy, seeing how she was taking this information.

Suddenly, she burst out laughing. "You homeboy, you."

He couldn't help but smile. "Johnno got a suspended sentence, I got my arse kicked by Dave. And Forrest always kept an eye on us after that."

They drove in silence then for a while, the tape still playing. Kiss, Motley Crue, Goons, Van Halen…Jason smiled every time another song started. He was feeling 17 again. The old Holden, tape turned up, girl dozing in the corner of the seat…Christ, who said time machines didn't exist?

He thought about Cheryl. Jason and Cheryl had known each other since they were five. They'd held hands in first grade and kissed in the third. They were a couple throughout childhood in that schoolyard 'love and marriage' teasing way kids have. But when they hit their teens, Cheryl's hormones burst the dam and she became a buxom, shapely lass well before her time while Jason stayed skinny, acne ridden and a boy. She preferred someone, anyone, older.

The night Johnno pulled his brother's rifle from the car changed all that. By association Jason suddenly had credibility, street cool, maturity and Cheryl started answering his calls.

He thought about what Forrest had told him. He'd said she had three kids now. There was almost a fourth. He wondered if anyone remembered. They'd pretty well kept the pregnancy a secret. His mum, her parents, he didn't think anyone else knew except maybe Forrest and probably the doctor. But then would he even remember? Just another miscarriage, another statistic, wash your hands, next patient please. Jason didn't even know if they'd lost a boy or a girl but, then, could you tell that early? They'd never talked about it in human terms.

After the incident with the gun, they became a couple. It was what Jason had always wanted. Of course it couldn't last. Cheryl got pregnant two days before her 17th birthday.

At first, neither of them wanted to believe it.

"You're just late."

"I'm never late, Jason. New moon, new blood... give or take a day or two."

They were sitting in Romeo's Pizza Bar. She picked off an olive. "I hate these black ones." She dropped it with the others on a side plate. "The new moon was two weeks ago."

"I know, I know." He pulled the core from his garlic bread. "So what do we do?"

"We get married, buy a house and raise a family, of course."

He coughed, wet bread splattering his sleeve. "You are joking, aren't you?"

She laughed, handed him a napkin. "Of course I am. My dad would never let me marry a Myers. He'd just say like father like son."

Jason wiped his arm. "Hey, c'mon I'm not that bad."

"Well, I guess not yet. But then I am 17 and pregnant to you so maybe you are following in his footsteps."

He shook his head. "If I was following in his footsteps I'd be halfway to Darwin right now, not sitting here admitting my part in this."

She picked off another olive. "Anyway, if I tell dad he'll just make me get rid of it."

"Would you?' he asked, "Get rid of it?"

"I really don't know." She looked embarrassed. "I don't love you Jason, you do know that, don't you?"

He could feel himself going red. "I know. But it's my baby, too."

"Do you want me to get rid of it?"

"I don't know." His voice squeaked. "I'm scared Cheryl, I'm not father material."

She put her hand on his. "You could be."

It was a moment he still remembered. Cheryl miscarried in the 11th week. They drifted apart pretty quickly, helped by her father declaring that if he ever saw that little Myers prick hanging around the house again he'd feed him to their German shepherds, Zoltan and Karloff.

After Cheryl he somehow fell in with Joanne, a girl he met at work. He liked her, she liked him, they enjoyed similar things, within months he found himself engaged. After that the marriage just seemed natural, the divorce maybe not. It still made his head spin to remember that within a year and a half he'd been almost a father, then a married man and finally a divorcee. Quite often he found himself wondering how life would have turned out if he and Joanne hadn't rushed things, both so eager and so young, both wanting to strike out on their own, prove their independence to friends and family. If they'd just taken their time, if they hadn't rushed into it, so eager to prove their maturity, to show that they were adults, independent of their families, so many ifs. But then he realised, he never would have moved to the city, met Cindy, fathered Hank. He guessed that maybe it was all supposed to happen this way, maybe this was all fated somehow.

He looked over at Cindy as she dozed to the sounds of T.Rex.

"Yeah," he said softly to himself, "this was the way it was meant to be."

Four

Cindy woke up as they pulled into Hay. "Where are we?"

"Hay."

"I said where are we?"

Jason looked at her, was she joking?

"We're in Hay. I've got a room booked at the Highway Inn."

"Oh. Sorry, I'm still half-asleep."

She made him stop at a chemist. "I need some needles."

"What do you tell them?" He was still very uncomfortable about this development.

"I tell them I'm a junkie." She laughed. "Relax, I tell them I'm diabetic."

She got out the car, poked her head back in the window. "They never ask. Look at me Jason, I'm no English rose. They know what it's for."

At the motel she went into the bathroom so he wouldn't have to watch. "Don't worry, I'll take it easy. I didn't realise it was so pure."

"You've got five minutes, then I come in to get you." She locked the door behind her. They were in Hay because this was the route Cindy's father had taken when he'd packed the family off to Queensland.

Hay, Coonabarabran, Dubbo, Tamworth, Lismore and up through the coast. It was an attempt at a holiday on the way, something to take the family's mind off the big move as they headed to Brisbane to restart their lives, to give Cindy a second chance.

Cindy wanted to follow the trail again, she wanted to retrace her steps in an attempt to find out why she'd done what she'd done, what had driven her rebellion and maybe to atone for the upheaval she'd forced upon her family at the time.

As they lay on the bed she said, "I'm sorry, Jason, but I need something. It just hurts too much. You have no idea what it's like."

He squeezed her hand. "It's okay. I'm just a bit nervous, I guess. I'm a beer drinker, bit of speed occasionally..." he sighed. "I'm way out of my depth here."

"You country boys…" she kissed him lightly on the cheek. "I'll be careful."

"So what did you do in Hay anyway?"

"Nothing I can really remember. Dad still wasn't talking to me at that stage." Cindy knew that wasn't entirely true. He wasn't talking, just shouting. "We really just passed straight through. Dad wanted to get to West Wyalong."

Jason stroked her cheek. "That's a long drive. Didn't think your old man had that stamina."

"He can be very stubborn. He'd decided that was the first night's stop and he was going to make it. I think we stopped here just so my brother Malcolm could be sick. He got carsick a lot."

They lay together quietly listening to the traffic noises outside. Laying her head on his chest she listened to the steady rhythm of his heart until she nodded off. Jason lay there, aware of her shape, her smell, her very presence, staring at the ceiling and wondering if life would ever be normal again.

He glanced at Cindy, so tiny, thin, so little of her. He should have realised that she was using. He'd just attributed her size to her illness, to the cancer but really she had that look, that junkie figure, the dark eyes, he should have known. He'd seen enough of them in his time. Hell they were always in his shop trading in records for money. How could he have missed it? He remembered the ratman. He hadn't thought about him for years. He was a big guy, beard hanging down, solid and tattooed. He always had a rat on his shoulder. Because Jason sold black metal records and a few Crowley books, the ratman would come in and espouse his theories on the occult and the devil. He seemed to know a lot too. There was something about his presence that made you listen to every word he said, something scary. "He knows things that people aren't supposed to know," was how Jason's employee and drinking buddy Josh put it. The ratman had a girlfriend. She was a scrawny little thing, all skin and bones; she was a junkie. *Ratman and rodent* he and Josh used to call them behind their backs. Never to their faces though, ratman would have beaten them to a pulp or worse, thought Jason, much worse. Jason realised that Cindy looked a lot like rodent now, at least physically. But then he thought, "I'm being a bit fucking harsh, she's got cancer, she's dying for Christ's sake, of course she's wasting away." He flinched.

"What else could she do?" he said out loud without realising it.

Cindy stirred, murmuring his name before rolling away and settling back to sleep. Jason watched her sleeping. He was still in love with her. He'd known it the night she told him she'd had enough, the night he'd agreed to take her home. He wanted to make up for everything else he'd put her through but now he didn't know if he was strong enough, if he was a decent enough man to be able to go through with this trip. He felt like he should cry but his face was dry. He pulled Cindy back to him, cuddling up to her gently, loving the familiarity of her texture, her smell and soon fell asleep.

They woke up early both feeling only mildly refreshed. Jason decided he was going to make pancakes. He nipped across the road and bought a shake and bake pack and some fake maple syrup.

As he cooked the pancakes the smell made him think of his father. It was one of the few memories he still had of his father. Every Sunday morning his dad would cook up a plate of pancakes and they'd all sit at the kitchen table and eat together. It was the only morning of the week that they'd all get together.

"Did your dad do pancakes?" he asked Cindy as she made them both coffees.

"Not really, why?"

"My dad used to make them every Sunday."

"Who? Dave?" She put the cups on the little breakfast bar.

"No, Frank, the old bastard who left me." He carefully flipped the pancakes onto a plate.

"It was one of the few rituals we had, one of the only days we all ate together."

He put the plate in front of her. "Dig in. They're not as good as the real thing but they'll do."

He sat down and poured syrup over his own stack. "We'd eat the pancakes and Frank would read the paper and mum would fuss about making coffee. It was good."

Cindy watched him talking. He rarely said anything about his real father. "So he wasn't all bad then?"

He shrugged. "I guess not. Bradley was hurt more than me. He was a bit older, it affected him more. I never really saw the old fart much anyway, but Bradley, he doted on Frank's attention."

"I've always wondered why you and Brad are so different. I mean you're such a fuck up…"

"Thanks honey, I love you too."

She smirked. "And he's in real estate, making the big dollars. You are both so different. Do you think that's what it was, your father leaving?"

Again, he shrugged. "Maybe. I think Bradley felt if he was successful, if he proved himself at sports and school and stuff then maybe Frank would come back."

He took a sip of his coffee. "I was just too shy to do any of that stuff. I just went into a fantasy world, you know, toys, music… I was trying to show that I didn't need him."

"Just in case he ever came back?"

"As if that was ever going to happen." He looked at his pancakes. "I did miss his pancakes though. We never really had them again. Dave is a crap cook."

Cindy pulled a face as she tasted her pancakes. "Well, stepfather or not he's definitely passed that trait on to you."

They left Hay feeling much better and ready to go. The road out was flat, plains stretching all around. Jason looked at the horizon, low and clear, and wondered what was ahead of him. He was determined to see this thing through now, the drugs made no difference. He'd made a promise to get Cindy home and he was going to keep that promise. He was going to prove that he was worthy, last night's doubts pushed deep into the back of his mind, he was strong enough and he was going to prove it.

He reached across and fished a tape out of the glove box, put it on and turned it up. It was Funhunt, his favourite band. Cindy had to smile. For a time it had seemed that whenever Funhunt played Jason would be found up the front, drunk and raucous, singing along and spilling his beer.

"You really used to love these guys, didn't you?"

"Shit yeah. Still do. Absolutely my favourite band."

"Why? What's so good about them?"

Jason looked at her, looked back at the road; he wasn't seeing the countryside now though, he was seeing the band. Vic prowling across the stage, swinging the microphone menacingly over the audience's heads, Kent hitting his guitar until his fingers bled and the crowd always pushing forward, dancing, throwing cans and insults, sweating and bleeding themselves. "It was like a gang I guess, a lifestyle."

He smiled to himself at the memories of being thrown off stage, of being told by Vic to stop writing Funhunt in blood on the pub walls. "When I saw Funhunt I felt like I was part of something. There were guys at those gigs I'd never see anywhere else. They only came out for Funhunt. We were all fuck-ups and losers, but at a Funhunt gig we were in control, we were the majority."

"A bonding experience huh? Why didn't you all just get tribal and set up a sweat lodge?"

"Laugh all you want, Funhunt shows were the one time I felt like I was part of something, like I knew what was happening."

Cindy laughed. "I was with you at some of those shows, you never knew what was happening."

Jason shook his head. "I might not remember every detail but I remember how I felt back then. I've never felt like that since."

"Never?"

"Okay, when Hank was born I definitely felt better but it wasn't like that. Hank's birth was a personal thing; Funhunt was a feeling of finally belonging somewhere."

Cindy squeezed his knee. "It's important to belong."

"To me it was I don't know that it is anymore." The music stopped mid-song. "It's not supposed to do that." Jason pushed the eject button, nothing happened.

"I think it's stuck."

"No shit Sherlock." He pushed the button again. Nothing. He jiggled the tape, felt some movement.

"Jason!" Cindy's voice was loud, fearful. He looked up, the car was drifting into the right lane.

"Shit, sorry." He slowed down, pulled over. He jiggled the tape again, hit the eject button, finally the cassette came out, tape unspooling like brown ribbon. "Fuck, fuck, fuck." He looked dejectedly at the cassette shell, its guts spilling into his lap.

"Well, I guess the party's over," said Cindy as she patted his leg. He wound down the window, threw the tape out across the highway, watching the brown innards flutter in the early morning breeze.

"It's alright, there's a back-up tape in my bag."

"You're kidding."

"I never kid about Funhunt."

Cindy fossicked through the glove box trying to find something else to put on.

"Hey, there's a Vacant Stare tape here," she said surprised.

He grinned. "Yeah, of course there is."

"I didn't think they'd ever got it together enough to record anything." She put the tape in.

"Josh gave it to me. They never released it."

The music kicked in, a loud raucous guitar noise that always grabbed everyone's attention at gigs. "Why didn't they release it?"

Jason was still grinning. "Too fucking drunk to get it finished properly. They had a label interested and everything but Josh couldn't get his shit together. Too many nights at Cassidy's."

"Ah yes… the infamous Cassidy's flat. You spent a lot of time there while I was away with Hank didn't you?"

Jason looked over at her. He could see that teasing smile of hers, the eyes flickering with mischief, just briefly, like they used to but he could see the pain too. Things hadn't quite seemed so funny back then when she'd first come back from Queensland to find Jason partying with Cassidy and the others.

"I knew you'd be back sometime."

Her eyes gleamed. "Oh did you just? So that girl you were fucking was just to pass the time?"

He glanced at her then back at the road. "She was there I guess… at the right time…"

He didn't know what to say. "Look it was just the way things happened. You'd gone, I didn't know when or if you were even coming back… you know, you get those times, those bursts of intensity, of action and you roll with them. Those few months you were away were like that. Cassidy's flat became party central, there was always something happening, gigs and people and music and we just rolled with it until it burnt out."

Jason wondered what she wanted, what she was after. "Look Cindy, we've been through that so many times. I fucked up. You weren't around, I didn't know what was happening with us…" He stopped. He really wanted to scream, "Hey it was you who attacked me with a fucking baseball bat!" but he didn't.

He could see the town limits ahead. He was happy for the distraction. "We're almost there and I'm kind of pooped. Can we just get into the room and talk about this later?"

But Cindy wasn't listening now. The sign had rekindled her own memories and all she was thinking about now was her first trip to West Wyalong, so many years ago.

Five

Cindy had celebrated her 15th birthday in West Wyalong. A Chinese restaurant if she remembered correctly. They'd stayed in a caravan park, her mum and dad in the double bed, curtained off, Malcolm and her getting the bunk beds. It was bad enough being in the car together for hours on end but being crammed in the caravan just seemed worse.

On her birthday they'd walked up the main street just in time for a street parade. It must have been the Christmas parade, she supposed, since her birthday fell in December. Or was it her brother's birthday? It didn't seem right that they were traveling so close to Christmas. No, she was sure it was her birthday; she could still remember the fight with her parents after the meal.

The parade itself seemed fairly short. Trucks went by, people she didn't know waved at other people she didn't know, lollies were thrown to the kids, clowns wandered around… she couldn't recall the appearance of Father Christmas though. Strange, she thought, surely I'd remember that.

Maybe they'd kept on walking before his big arrival, she couldn't remember. The food at the restaurant was okay, nothing to write home about, if she knew where home was, but it was okay.

She couldn't recall what, if any, presents she received. Possibly it was just money, they were traveling after all. Having a birthday so close to Christmas always meant missing out. Her friends always assumed she got lots of stuff with her birthday and Christmas being so close together, but in truth the presents always seemed to be halved.

One year, when she was eight, the family was so caught up in getting ready for Christmas they clean forgot her birthday. She said nothing, just waited until her mother finally came in at bedtime with a hastily wrapped present and a small apology. By her 15th birthday she no longer expected anything, maybe that was why she couldn't remember.

After the meal they walked back to the caravan park. The parade was over and she remembered stepping over lollies and streamers, pausing to examine a plastic mask someone had dropped. It was a pig, pink rosy cheeks, little ears sticking up. She gave it to Malcolm. He kept it for the rest of the trip, wearing it in the car every day which wouldn't have been so bad, she thought, if he wasn't 11½ years old.

Back at the caravan they'd all sat around the small table watching TV while her father looked over the road maps and planned the next day's journey. Her mum was drinking coffee, her dad had a beer.

Cindy sat quietly hoping he wouldn't want another. He did though and that's when the shouting started. She'd got him the first one so he hadn't looked in the fridge, but when he got up for the second she shrunk in her seat and braced herself.

"Hey, where's the other can? There should be another one left." He turned looking at the three of them.

Her mother said, "I don't know, dear, it certainly wasn't me."

Malcolm's pig face blinked, said nothing, just turned to Cindy. Her father stepped the one step from fridge to table, looked at Cindy. "Well?"

She was red in the face, could feel a trickle of sweat running down her back. There was no point in lying. "I drank it." She bowed her head. "While you and mum were out this afternoon."

"You did what? What the hell did you think you were doing?" His hands were resting on the table, pressing down, knuckles white. She watched them, waiting for the first sign of movement.

"I was thirsty, I wanted a drink," she answered quietly. His hands didn't move.

"You were thirsty? And water didn't occur to you? Coke maybe?"

"I wanted a beer." She knew she shouldn't have said it but she did. "I was hot, I was sick of being crammed in with Malcolm and you two and I wanted a fucking beer."

She didn't even see the hand move. He slapped her hard across the cheek. "You ungrateful little bitch. This whole trip is for you. This move is to give you another chance."

He pointed to her brother. "Young Malcolm didn't get expelled, you did. Remember that."

Cindy sneered. "Malcolm's too dumb to get expelled, unless they catch him playing with himself in the toilets."

Her mother slapped her from the other side. "Young lady, I don't know what's gotten into you but this is just too much." Cindy sat there, both cheeks tingling, her father's handprint still clearly visible but she refused to cry.

"I didn't want this trip, you did. This isn't about giving me a new start… it's about your embarrassment." She stood up, pushing Malcolm aside. "You're ashamed of what I've done to your name, of what I've done to your social standing. You haven't even asked me how I feel though."

She tried to get to the door but her father grabbed her arm. "Of course I'm ashamed. You should be, too. Do you know what you've put your mother and me through, do you?"

He pushed her towards the bunk beds. "This isn't over, young lady." She sat down narrowly missing her head on the upper bunk. "We all need a good night's sleep, it's a long drive tomorrow."

He looked down at Cindy. "And you need to start thinking about other people besides yourself." She sat there waiting for something else, a slap, another remark, punishment of some kind but there was nothing. He simply turned off the television and disappeared behind the curtain.

Her mother stood up, eyes wet and followed him. Malcolm sat at the table, pig mask still on, trying to pick his nose through the small breathing holes. Cindy didn't even bother to undress, just slid under the blankets and cried into her pillow.

Now, as her and Jason were approaching West Wyalong, she wondered if the restaurant would still be there or the caravan park. And then she started wondering what had happened in the end to that damn pig mask.

Six

Cindy was asleep so Jason slipped out for a quick beer. He didn't like leaving her alone but she seemed okay, sleeping quite peacefully, a hint of a smile on her face so he'd decided a quick drink couldn't hurt.

He was standing in the front bar quietly nursing a schooner when two blokes sidled up next to him and ordered. One was a big, blonde boofhead, like an old-fashioned full back, the other was smaller but solid, balding, faded tattoos running up both arms.

"Jeez, I needed that one, Col, you want another?"

"Does the Pope shit in the woods? No, it's alright, my shout, Ralphy."

Colin turned to Jason. "You want one, mate? You look like a bloke with a thirst."

Jason smiled. "No, that's okay. Thanks for the offer but I'm pacing myself."

"So are we, mate, we're just running a bit faster is all."

Ralph offered his hand. "Name's Ralph Dunleavy and this is my mate Colin Wolfe."

"Jason Myers."

Col turned, two fresh schooners in his generous mitts. He handed a beer to Ralph and Jason noticed he was missing two fingers.

"So you a local, Jason?"

He shook his head. "No, just passing through on my way up the coast."

He looked at Col. "You?"

"No, mate, but I hope to be." He looked at Ralph who nodded. "Ralph and me are up here prospecting."

"Prospecting?"

Ralph stepped closer and Jason realised his left eye was glass.

"Gold, mate, this place used to be big…"

"And we reckon there's still more out there," interrupted Col, "just gotta be prepared to work for it."

"So why aren't there others doing it?"

"Like I said, mate, you gotta work for it."

Col finished his beer, wiped his mouth. "Another?"

Ralph nodded, handed over his glass and looked at Jason. "You in?"

Jason blinked. "What? The gold?"

"No, mate, the beer. Though if you're willing to work you can always come with us."

Colin laughed. "Yeah we could do with someone with two eyes and 10 fingers. You're not missing any toes, are ya?"

They found a table and sat down. Jason bought a round. "So how long you two been doing this?"

"Just started. Came up last week."

"Yeah," said Colin, "got a camp set up at the caravan park and we're just planning our next move."

"And you reckon there's gold out there."

Ralph shrugged. "Why not? There was once, they can't have got it all." He paused for a drink. "Just gotta find it is all."

"And we got nothin' else to do. Hard to get labourin' jobs with a coupla fingers missing."

Jason wondered whether he should ask. Col saved him the trouble.

"Lost 'em on my last job. Farmer's labourer, doin' some fencin' and I got tangled. Straight off they came, fuck it 'urt." He looked at the gap between his index and little fingers, wiggling the stumps. "I was workin' for cash, too. No compo just an extra week's pay to tide me over."

"Can they do that?" asked Jason.

"They can do anything they want," said Ralph, "we don't exist anymore mate, the working class just don't exist."

Colin nodded. "Ralphy's right. There's no bloody work and too many of us to do it. I'm off the farm, 10 minutes later they got someone else to replace me. Me bloody fingers are under some fence post but they don't care." He slumped in his chair. "We're disposable."

Ralph got up and went to the bar. He came back with a jug. "Works out cheaper. Gotta budget you know." He poured the drinks slowly. "I gotta get the depth right. I miss sometimes."

"Usually after a few beers," chipped in Col as he took his glass. He looked around the bar. "You know, I don't mind this place. Reckon even if we don't strike it rich, I might stay."

After another round, Jason realised he'd better get back to Cindy. He'd only intended to slip out for one beer and he'd been gone over an hour. "Sorry, fellas gotta go. Nice meeting you."

He shook hands with both and stood to leave. Ralph stood, too. "If you're ever looking for some work, young Jason, we'll be here."

"You never know, Ralph, you never know."

As Jason crossed the street he thought about what was waiting for him at home: a part-time factory job, a one bedroom ex-Housing Trust flat, the girl from accounts he saw once or twice a month…it didn't look promising really. "You never know, Ralph."

Cindy was still asleep, still smiling. She still looks good, he thought, a bit dark around the eyes, a bit gaunt but still essentially as pretty as when he'd first seen her.

He remembered the first time he'd caught her eye at the pub, at a Funhunt gig. He'd been watching her most of the night as she flitted around, dropping ice down people's backs, poking and prodding friends and generally being a nuisance. She'd turned, saw him staring, smiled and waving an empty glass mouthed, "Drink, please."

He happily obliged and they started talking. Or rather, she started jabbering and he nodded, smiled and wondered what the hell kind of drugs she was on. He found out later she was on nothing but mild psychosis and a rebellious streak. She was determined to 'kick out the jams' and fuck with the status quo. He gladly went along for the ride, if somewhat cautiously.

It was a relationship based solely on sex, alcohol and her trying to shock him. He still remembered the night they first went to bed together. It seemed funny after but he knew they'd been very lucky that night. Lucky they'd just been asked to leave the pub; no strong-arm tactics, no police, just leave. Everyone was so touchy about blood then, he guessed they probably still were now. She did look pretty bizarre though, inverted cross in red on her forehead, 666 on her cheek, blood smeared over her chin. He remembered how it all started. He'd dropped his glass and when he picked it up, he'd sliced his finger open. Nothing major but enough to cut through the alcoholic daze and make him feel it. Cindy had taken his finger gently in her hand and then suckled on the blood. He wondered if she was trying to shock him but strangely enough it didn't. When she cut her own finger though to return the favour he had to admit she did manage to at least make him pause. Later on he thought it strange that their first physical contact should be feasting on each other's blood but at the time he didn't think at all just react. And that was all Cindy ever really wanted - reaction. She doted on it, lived for it. Everything she did seemed geared to make people react, to make them think for just a moment about their situation, about their space, nothing was as it seemed with her. That was what he liked about her, that maniacal energy and tension that always made life, well, more interesting. He looked forward to seeing her, to being with her, watching, listening, soaking up some of that energy, that zeal. It wasn't even primarily sexual, a first for Jason. No, it was the exuberance for life, the pace, the frivolity, and the enjoyment she was having, living. The sheer irresponsibility of it all that was what drew him to her. The way she could make something happen, some moment, out of nothing. The blood being a perfect example of that. When she'd requested he draw the upside-down cross on her forehead, her voice squeaky with excitement and alcohol, it just seemed like the right thing to do. They probably could have kept on cutting and suckling, feeding off each other, if they hadn't smeared 666 and a very poorly drawn pentagram on the wall. That was when the barman told them to leave. Immediately. No sense of humour.

They left the pub, wandered down to a taxi rank, still covered in blood and waited. Jason remembered that he almost got into a fight with a guy who didn't seem to see the funny side of the situation but then a cab pulled up and Cindy dragged him in before blows could be thrown. Jason had lent out the window, determined to have the last word and copped a smack across the chops. They went back to her place and had sex for the first time. And for the first but not the last time she made him bleed.

It felt good too, and that had surprised him. He'd never seen himself as someone who was in to rough sex but that first night she had introduced him to something inside him that he hadn't known existed, a darker side maybe. Despite his being older he was still the naïve country kid really. You got the girl, you fucked, and you got a beer after.

But Cindy was different, she wanted something out of this exchange of bodily fluids, she wanted a piece of you. And Jason was more than willing to offer himself to her.

That was what it was like, he thought, we gave pieces of ourselves to each other, we swapped the pain for pleasure. He often wondered just what had caused so much pain in her though, for she was always the instigator always the one trying to push through the pain barrier. He wondered now how much of that pain he had ended up instilling in her, how much of it all was his fault. At the time he didn't think like that though, he just lapped it all up, enjoying the moment, the ride, the intensity of their early nights together. Like moths crashing into the flame, getting burnt over and over and coming back for more. He didn't think he'd ever felt more alive than those first few months together.

All he really wanted was to relive those first days again. To be lying on her mattress in the cool of the morning, the shades drawn and the air stale with the smell of last night, beer, sex and cigarettes. He wanted to be able to reach over for that glass of water she always kept on the floor on her side of the bed. He wanted to feel her body next to him as he lapsed back into sleep, dozing on and off till the morning sun warmed the room and he could rise naked, without goose bumps and stumble out through the kitchen to the back yard and piss away that last beer. Then padding back to the fridge, he'd see if there were any beers left. If there were he'd take one in and sit on the mattress watching her sleep while he sipped at his morning eye opener. He liked to watch her sleeping. She always looked so peaceful and calm, totally unlike her manic and constantly busy state when awake. But that wasn't possible now, not anymore. Playtime was over and had been for a long time now. He looked at her now, she still looked peaceful and calm, still looked like his Cindy. But he knew she wasn't anymore. Maybe she never had been his Cindy.

When Cindy fell pregnant with Hank, things changed. She stopped being so wild but it seemed to Jason that he took over. Cindy had settled down after Hank's birth but Jason hadn't. She'd opened up a door in him that he wasn't willing to close just yet. He was singing in a band, bedding girls, drinking, fighting, it was like all his teenage dreams had been fulfilled. He loved Hank but he couldn't accept the responsibility of fatherhood just yet. He and Cindy had said that the relationship wasn't supposed to be serious and he kept her to her word. Jason didn't think he was ready and then, when he finally was, when they'd finished the fighting, the push me-pull you, when they'd healed the wounds and decided to settle together, to give their son a life they both felt they'd missed out on; when Jason had finally matured enough to be a father, a partner, possibly a husband, Hank ran out in front of a white Toyota Corolla, chasing the ball Jason had thrown too hard, too fast. He died instantly. The driver had to be sedated; he never got behind the wheel again.

Without Hank as their glue, Cindy and Jason soon fell apart. Somehow Cindy stayed strong but Jason went headlong back into the hedonistic lifestyle of booze and girls. He was amazed at Cindy's tolerance, after all she was supposed to be the crazy, wacky one in this relationship. She didn't stay tolerant for long though. That first Christmas without Hank was too much, it was over. The shop soon became too much for him too and after that he drifted into menial work and meaningless relationships. He would wake up with a hangover and occasionally a girl by his side, shower, get dressed and start again. He was chasing something, ego boost, recognition, a reason maybe but all he got was further down the work ladder and alcohol-induced blackouts.

When Cindy was first diagnosed it barely registered. He was in a self-destructive relationship with a young singer who liked being dominated while still pretending to family and friends she was the Virgin Mary. He always wondered how she explained the scars and welt marks but he didn't dwell too long on it. Cindy's cousin Greg rang him to tell him about the cancer; Cindy still wasn't talking to him. Jason muttered some pleasantries, promised to visit her in hospital and then climbed back into bed with the Virgin Queen.

When she got sick of his drinking interfering with their sex life and dumped him for an ambulance driver he wallowed in misery for five days and nights before realising that, really, he just didn't give a fuck. He was living in a one-bedroom concrete block with a view of six other concrete blocks, working as a casual store man in a furniture shop and drinking himself to sleep every night of the week. He was pathetic and he finally realised it. He called Cindy and arranged to visit her. Seeing her in a hospital bed, a drip hanging from her arm, her head in bandages was the jolt Jason needed to get back to some form of reality. It scared him that he had been so blasé about her diagnosis, that he probably wouldn't have got around to visiting her if the Virgin Mary hadn't dumped him.

He realised then that he really didn't like himself that was why he needed others, why he was always trying to get laid. He just wanted someone else to like him, to justify his existence because he couldn't anymore.

He gradually weaned himself back to three or four days of drinking and only a couple of nights of serious bingeing, started eating better and stopped chasing skirt. He would go and see Cindy every few days and make sure she was okay. He found a weight bench in the classifieds and started exercising, bought some new shirts, lost some weight. He felt good about himself and realised that was what he was looking for. He no longer needed confirmation from other people, he liked himself now.

Of course that wasn't completely true. There was one person he still needed and he wished he knew how to tell her that. And he wished she wasn't dying on him.

47

Seven

When Cindy woke in the morning, the sun peeking through the curtains trying in vain to warm the room, Jason was slumped in a chair snoring, a can of beer leant against his chest.

Just like the old days, she thought. She felt good this morning. She had days like this occasionally, where the disease had a rest and let her, momentarily at least feel alive and fresh. She checked the bedside clock, breakfast was due in 20 minutes. Should she wake him? She decided to have a quick shower instead.

Cindy stood under the shower enjoying the hot spray as it washed over her. The good old days she thought. Were they that good? It seemed so long ago, they were different people now, Jason and her. She never would have imagined that she would be here with him now, disease or not. It had been a fling, a bit of fun with the older guy who owned the record shop, that was the plan, the idea. It was never meant to be any more than that but somehow he had hung around, he'd dug himself in and it slowly became more. And it wasn't just Hank it was something else. There was something about this man, this dropkick adolescent in a grown up's body that she found interesting, that she liked, maybe even had loved. Funny how these things happen. She stepped out and grabbed a towel. She remembered when he turned up one day at her house with a toothbrush and a towel. "I figured I was spending so much time here I better have some basics on hand," he'd said as he waltzed into her bathroom. That was when she knew he was serious. Well, as serious as he could be considering neither of them would admit to anything other than a convenient lust for each other. She grinned, what a strange ride it had been. She never could have envisaged this, never foreseen that they would be here now. Even if she could have seen her future, their future she wouldn't have believed it. She wrapped herself in her towel and opened the bathroom door.

When she came out he was standing in the middle of the room, a wet patch down his front, swearing. The beer can lie on the floor, a small pool of beer around it.

"You'll find some tissues in my bag," she said smiling. Just like the good old days.

Over breakfast, toast, Weet-Bix and instant coffee, he told her about Ralphy and Colin.

"So do you think they'll find any gold?"

"I don't know. I doubt it but like they said, there was once." He shrugged, took a bite of toast. "Maybe they're onto something, maybe not."

She buttered her toast. "I wonder why no one else has thought of it?"

"Guess no one has been desperate enough yet. Can't be any worse than some of the jobs I've had lately though."

"So why don't you join them?"

He sipped his coffee, it was bitter, lukewarm. "I just might yet, you never know."

After breakfast Cindy decided she wanted a tour of the town. She knew this energy wouldn't last so she wanted to enjoy it, to get out in the fresh air, to look around. She wanted to chase some ghosts away.

They walked along the main street, the autumn sun slowly warming them. She wondered out loud if the Christmas parade was still held.

"So," said Jason, "has it changed much?"

"I don't really remember too much. It was 15 years ago." She pointed at the DVD store. "But I'm guessing that wasn't here."

"Tell me again, why did your old man come through this way?"

Cindy blushed slightly. "Because I was a bitch. He was trying to create a family atmosphere, bond us together."

"By coming the long way?" he laughed.

"It was a holiday, you prick, haven't you ever had a holiday?"

"Not after the old boy left. By the time Dave wooed my mum Bradley and I were a little too set in our ways for family holidays."

"You didn't miss much." She stopped, looked around. "I think the restaurant was down that way."

They walked on, stopping to look in the windows and enjoying the sun's warmth.

"So why were you a bitch? Your olds don't seem that bad."

She looked at him. He was smiling. She punched him in the arm. "No, they're not that bad. I am just a bitch, I guess." She stopped. "I really don't know."

Cindy gazed blankly into the shop window. She had spent the past few months looking back over those years, assessing, dissecting, pulling her teenage years apart like Lego blocks and reassembling; trying to make some sense of it all, trying in vain to work out what it was she'd been rebelling against but she couldn't recall any moment or anything that had made her do what she did, made her become the person she had become.

Her parents hadn't been all that bad, her life was a comfortable middle-class existence. Dad ran a sports shop, Mum did canteen duty, there was always money, the kids never went short on anything, but Cindy had something inside of her, driving her, pushing her to rebel, react, to fight against the comfort of her life but she wasn't sure why. She couldn't explain it, she just did it, like a Nike spokesperson for the bad things in life. Drugs, booze, sex – just do it!

"I just didn't like being normal, I guess. There's something about the status quo that bugs me, that whole family and kids and work and holidays and all that."

Still, she thought, there must be something. For a second she had a flash, her mother in tears maybe or was it Cindy? She could taste copper in her mouth, on her tongue, she swallowed but nothing went down. There was something there, some memory, a moment she was trying to recall but then Jason interrupted her train of thought and it was gone.

She frowned. "Sorry, what did you say?"

He tapped his head. "I was just asking if you maybe got dropped on your head as a baby?"

"No, I didn't," she laughed, "but your mum told me you did."

"Did she tell you I was a month late?"

"What do you mean?"

"I mean, I stayed in…they had to induce me. I wasn't coming out."

"What did they use? Beer?"

"Yeah, very funny." They walked on. "Anyway, it's true, I was late. Came out red raw, like a skinned rabbit. Mum reckons her body was in the process of consuming me, of digesting me, that's why my skin was peeling, acid or something."

"So you've always been stubborn."

"And late." They stopped outside a deli. "Fancy anything?" Jason asked.

"I've got a chocolate craving actually, something sweet."

He went in, bought a block of fruit'n'nut and a Coke. "There you go, princess. By the way who do I send the bill to?"

She took the chocolate, started unwrapping it. "What do you mean? You asked me if I wanted anything?"

He pulled out his wallet, opened it. "Well, until my holiday pay goes in the bank, this is pretty much it and that's for petrol. Next town is on you."

Cindy broke off a row of chocolate, popped it in her mouth, loving the rush of taste and the slickness of the chocolate. "Don't worry we won't run out."

"You might not, I'm not so sure about me."

"Well, you'll just have to go back on the street, won't you?"

He laughed, accepted a row of fruit'n'nut. "I thought we wanted to make money."

Cindy ran her hand across his chest. It felt good. "I'm sure some lonely girl would pay for this."

Jason felt goose bumps rising on his arms. He looked at her, smiled ruthlessly.

"How much you got, lonely girl?"

They ran back to the motel, giggling like teenagers.

It was a strange moment for both of them. They hadn't slept together for a long time and they'd both changed physically. Both had lost weight but Jason had gained muscle tone, firmed up while Cindy had faded away. She kept her shirt on and pulled the sheet over herself. She wanted Jason but she didn't want him to see her naked now, to see what was left of her.

Jason, on the other hand, wanted to show her how healthy he looked now. He wanted her to see his arms, his chest, to comment on his new physique, on how good he was looking. She couldn't. Too self-conscious of her own body she barely noticed his. The sex was frantic, quick – they both needed the release – then they did it again, slower this time, the demons having been momentarily chased away.

The whole time though Jason was scared he would break her, that she would crumble in his arms, like dried leaves, down to dust and debris, skeletal remains of a vibrant life swept aside in clumsiness and coitus. It was probably the gentlest he'd ever been.

They were cuddled up on the bed, watching the midday movie, some early Tarzan flick when Cindy started crying. Jason sat quietly not knowing what to do, what to say. Should he ask her or should he wait for her to tell him? The sobbing got softer, slowed. Then, dabbing at her eyes with a tissue, she said quietly, "Thank you."

Closing her eyes she went to sleep in his arms. Jason stared at the monkey on the TV as it cavorted through the trees. He wiped a tear from his cheek and waited for Tarzan to stop the elephant stampede.

Eight

Cindy wanted to find the Chinese restaurant. They were heading off in the morning so it had to be now, despite the rain. Rugged up, covered in jumper and hat, gloves and scarf, Jason thought she looked like a scarecrow, albeit an emaciated one but he wouldn't dare say it to her face.

"Okay, which way?" he asked as they left their room.

"There was a side street, past the DVD shop. I think it's down there."

Huddled together, they dashed from canopy to roof trying to stay dry, dodging puddles, umbrellas and fellow travelers. Soon they stood outside the DVD shop.

"Okay, now what?"

Cindy pointed to a street sign. "That way, I think."

"You think?"

"It was a long time ago but I think it's down there." She shook her head, droplets of water flying off her hat. "We walked up the main street, turned down a side street and there it was."

"You trying to convince me or you?" They walked on but there was no sign of the restaurant.

"Just a little further." Cindy could feel the water getting in under her hat, dripping down her neck. She wondered if Jason was as cold and wet as she felt. They kept walking, looking down side streets and alleys but they couldn't find it.

"Come on, Cindy, let's get back. It ain't here any more."

She shook her head. "No, I've got to find it. It's here somewhere."

He stopped. "Just ask someone then."

"No! I have to find it, Jason. I don't want help."

She kept walking. They turned the next corner, nothing.

Jason took her arm, gently pulled her undercover. "Forget it, Cindy, it's gone. We're wet, cold, hungry and anyway, I don't even like Chinese food." He pulled her in close, feeling her shivering. Tears mingled with rain.

"I need to find it, I need to find it."

They stood there together; Cindy huddled to his chest repeating her mantra until the rain eased. Jason led her back to the motel, put her to bed and ordered a pizza. In the morning they headed off. Before they even passed the town limits, Cindy was asleep.

Cindy rarely remembered her dreams anymore, not since the chemotherapy. Before that she could always tell you in minute detail every moment and nuance of her dreams, every colour, every word, she remembered everything. She missed that, she missed her dream world; it had always been a place she could fall back on when she wasn't enjoying herself in this world. On this trip she had been determined to remember her dreams again, she wanted to take pleasure in every moment she had left and that included sleep. Slowly she had begun to fight back and recall her dreamscapes. She noticed that Jason seemed to feature a lot, as did her father. Jason always seemed to be there to stop her doing stupid things – jumping into mosh pits, wrestling crocodiles, sleeping with the Hawthorn football club. (She still hadn't forgiven him for that one.) The figure of her father though was harder to pin down. Sometimes he would be standing behind a shop counter serving her, other times he would just appear, mutter a few words about responsibility and disappear again. Once he'd quoted Anton La Vey and Henry Miller before donning a frilly apron and serving raw meat to a table full of strangers.

As she slept on the drive to Dubbo she was remembering something real though, something she didn't want to recall. She was dreaming of the day she attacked Jason with the baseball bat.

She was standing outside his flat, bouncing from foot to foot like boxers do before a fight. In her hand she held the bat. It had been a present for Hank from her parents. He'd never got to use it but she had. Jason's car was covered in paint, it dripped down the panels, stained the seats. All the windows were smashed in, the headlights too.

Dream Cindy seemed bigger, more muscles maybe and her smile seemed more maniacal, vicious even. Her teeth were like fangs and she licked her lips as she waited for Jason to come out of his flat and see the car. She would have rather found Nancy and beat on her with the bat but she didn't know where she lived. No one would tell her after the New Years Eve party. Not after she'd attacked the band and Amy. And especially not after she'd broken into Cassidy's flat looking for Jason.

Cindy stirred in the seat, moaning softly. Jason glanced over at her. He'd just passed through Forbes, home of Ben Hall whoever the hell he was and he really needed a piss break. He was scared to stop though, he didn't want to wake Cindy. She'd looked so exhausted this morning, barely eating anything, he wasn't even sure if she'd shot up but then again, he thought, she probably had found the strength to do that.

"Fuck," he muttered, "I'm getting to be a bitter old man."

Cindy was looking in his window now, hoping for some movement, some sign of life. Surely he'd heard the sound of the windows breaking. Everyone else had. In these flats though, no one asked questions. One or two heads popped out, dark, faceless then closed their doors and disappeared. She noticed the doors had sealed over with bricks now. Dream Cindy flicked out her tongue, tasting the fear in the air. She knew he was in there. He hadn't come out for a week now not since the last fight, the night he'd taken her to the hospital, the night she beat him up. That was nothing though, grunted Dream Cindy. This time it's for keeps. She swung the bat at the window. It disintegrated. Then she clubbed the walls. Bricks started to crumble, fall, piece by piece she blew his brick house down. "No," Cindy said to herself, "This isn't the way it happened." She tried to stop him coming out, tried to wish him away. Then the scene changed. Jason was standing naked at Hank's grave. He was holding a bouquet. Dream Cindy was sneaking up behind him, still swinging the baseball bat. But now she was dressed like one of the Baseball Furies from The Warriors movie. Jason didn't even scream, just fell on to the grave, the flowers still in his hand.

Cindy woke with a start.

"You okay?" Jason was sitting behind the wheel. He was dressed, there was no blood dripping from his forehead, there were no flowers crushed in his hand.

"Where are we?" she asked.

"Just coming into Parkes. I'm going to stop for a piss and a coffee. Do you want anything?"

She shook her head. "No. Just be quick. I don't want to be alone."

She fell asleep again as soon as they were back on the highway. She didn't have any more dreams.

Nine

Jason sipped his coffee as he drove. He was thinking about Nancy. It seemed so long ago, like it was another Jason who had led that life, another Cindy. He couldn't reconcile the girl dozing in the seat next to him with the woman who had come back from Brisbane four years ago, son in tow expecting everything to go on as it had. He wondered where Nancy was now, he wondered what might have been if he'd stayed with her, if Cindy hadn't finally snapped and attacked him, if he hadn't forgiven her. So many ifs and buts in life, so many what could have beens, should have beens but then his life was a series of could have beens, of what ifs and maybes. If his father had stayed around, if his marriage to Joanne hadn't failed, if Hank was still alive… he suddenly felt tired, drained. He wanted just to be back at the bar, back at the flat, anywhere but on this trip, anywhere but here taking Cindy home to die. He thought again about Nancy, about her fiery red hair, her pale skin, the trail of freckles down her spine. She had been the complete opposite of Cindy, he wondered now if that had been the attraction. He couldn't say. He'd told Cindy so many times since then that it was just a fling, that it had just happened because… well, because it did, because it could. He didn't know any more if he was telling the truth or not. He didn't know now what he had felt. He had just run with it, taken what had come his way and not even thought about the damage he would cause. Just like he'd always done, always believing that he was indestructible, infallible, that nothing could go wrong. Maybe that was why he was so forgiving afterwards, because in the end it felt like he'd brought the whole thing upon himself.

He thought back to the flat. Jason could still remember the first time he walked into Cassidy's flat. He took one sweeping look and said, "This is so fucking Bukowski."

There were 8 flats in the block, four downstairs, four on top. Access was gained to No. 6 via a set of stairs at the back, next to the communal laundry room. The laundry was perpetually damp and stank of old towels and moldy

57

soap. He never saw anyone in there, except once when he interrupted the junkie from No. 2 in the middle of a deal. She just looked up, smiled and went back to her business. The dealer, with his pants around his ankles, didn't say anything nor did he smile. At the top of the stairs, you had a choice of two doors, No. 6 or No. 8. For some reason Nos. 5 and 7 used the front stairwell. Cassidy's flat had two bedrooms, a shower and toilet, a tiny kitchen that looked down on the laundry and a lounge room through which you stepped out onto a balcony. Cass chose No. 6 because of that balcony. It was the best one of the lot, at least half was still useable. At No. 8 you had to tiptoe out over the gaps, and even then it could only hold one person's weight. Cassidy's balcony though could hold three plus a small esky. As long as you didn't go near the right hand corner. Cassidy's flat mate Mark did it once and after they pulled him back up and checked to make sure his leg was okay, they put an old cot across the far end as a barrier. Mark worked at 'Vinnies' and could always get furniture and knick-knacks cheap. Neither Mark nor Cassidy had beds just mattresses. They had spares for all their friends too, courtesy of Vinnies of course. Mark would pay for two and, loading the truck himself, take four. There were nine mattresses in the flat, the other three he sold. They were lined up in the hallway. It was like entering a low budget asylum. Coming back from the pub they would bounce from one side to the other trying to knock them down so the drunks behind would have to crawl over top of them. In the lounge were arranged a motley assortment of armchairs, deck chairs and a love seat, all courtesy of Mark. There was one large, brown coffee table in the middle of the room, the top of which couldn't be seen for CDs, records, magazines, bongs, video slicks and beer cans. In one corner sat the TV. It was perpetually on. No one really watched it; it was just left on. They'd go to the video shop and rent the cheapest, dumbest looking movies they could find and just leave them playing. Old zombie flicks, flashdance rip-offs, stalker movies, Chuck Norris videos… it didn't matter, they were just background movement. Next to the TV was the stereo, Cassidy's pride and joy. A 1972 quadraphonic unit with a CD player precariously rewired through the back. Records lay all over the floor in front of it, covers piled up on top of the speakers. In a box were some 2000 singles, courtesy of Cassidy's relentless pursuit of every pop song known, and occasionally unknown, to man. Thursday nights they'd sit around drinking while Cassidy played records and everyone tried to guess who they hell they were. It was very educational.

Jason laughed quietly. What a bunch of overgrown teenagers. How the hell did any of them ever get girls? One look at that flat should have been enough to scare them off. Cindy stirred and he glanced over. Of course she hadn't been around much then. Cindy was probably the only girl that could have appreciated the whole mess. If she hadn't had her own mess to deal with.

"Hey kiddo, nice nap?"

She stretched and yawned. "I'm sorry. I'm just so tired today."

Jason shrugged his shoulders. "It's not a problem. Although I get a bit dozy myself without someone to keep me company." He turned down the tape deck. "You were moaning there early on. Bad dreams?"

Cindy didn't know what to say. Should she tell him about the dream? "It was nothing really. Just a bit of a flashback I guess."

He nodded and took another sip of coffee. It was cold now but he didn't know what to do with it. "Yeah, was just having one of those myself."

She looked over to him happy that he was here, that he wasn't slumped on the ground with Dream Cindy standing over him. "What about?"

Jason wasn't sure what to say. It wasn't a time they liked to talk about much or share. "Nothing really. Just keeping my mind ticking over I guess."

"You were thinking about Nancy weren't you?" Cindy said. Her voice, though quiet, dripped with venom.

She shivered. Were there fangs in her mouth right now? Was this still a dream?

He was shaking his head, maybe too vigorously she thought. "No, no… about Cassidy's and stuff that's all."

Cassidy's place, always it came back to Cassidy's. She'd gone away and he'd replaced her with that place she thought bitterly. And with those people.

No, she thought, that wasn't fair. They'd always been there, it wasn't his fault, what else was he going to do?

Cindy tried to lighten up the mood. "Tell me about the Jimmy Lancaster night. You've never told me the whole thing I don't think."

He almost breathed a sigh of relief. "You sure? It's a long story."

She reached over and touched his hand. "We've got plenty of time. And it will help keep me awake."

Jason smiled and put on his best voice. "Well, as you know Cassidy worked in the storeroom of a bookshop and got regular invitations to launches and lunchtime soirees. The dry, intellectual affairs he'd usually avoid but once in a while there'd be some young talent, some new author with their finger on the *'youth culture'* pulse and those launches would at least have lots of beer and girls. They were the shows we would go to. Cassidy, Mark and me usually, sometimes Josh as well."

"Why wasn't Josh involved? Did you have a lovers tiff?" He could tell she was starting to enjoy herself now. There was some of the old fire building up. He liked seeing it in her.

"Nah, it was his turn to open the shop I think. We took the hangovers in turn."

He slowed down behind a truck, waiting until it was safe to pass.

"Anyway, back to the story. On this night it was the local launch of Jimmy Lancaster's *Titanium Trousers*, a book about rock'n'roll or something. The bar was open, there was a reasonable buffet and there were bands playing. The whole youth culture vibe was happening. Lancaster had been roadie for Powderfinger or You Am I or some Triple J band for a week or two and wrote this book about his insight into the life of a rock band on the road."

She interrupted, poking him in the arm. "Such a cynic."

"And you like Powderfinger?"

"Okay you got me there." She waved her hand like the queen, getting into the moment now, happy to be distracted. "Continue with the lies."

"Well, I went up to Jimmy, shook his hand, congratulated him on his efforts and headed to the bar. Cassidy followed close behind. Mark however cornered Jimmy and proceeded to question him on the validity of rock music as a movement of rebellion in the new millennium. Mark had been to see his shrink that morning and had got himself a new course of pills and they seemed to be working well."

Cindy interrupted again. "What were they?"

"I don't know you'd have to ask Mark. Actually you'd have to find him first. He's disappeared off the face of the earth." Another truck, he slowed again.

"You just mean he doesn't go to the pub anymore."

"That too." He accelerated and overtook, getting back into the lane just as the Ute came over the hill.

"Watch it Jason, I want to get to there in one piece."

"Don't sweat it we had plenty of room." He looked back in his mirror, there was a hand waving out of the Ute's window giving him the finger. "Same to you mate," he muttered to himself. "Anyway, where was I? Oh yes at the bar with Cassidy. The literary crowd was being very polite, sipping their light beers, nibbling the finger food but the small group of us associated with the music side of the biz…"

"And the freeloaders," she butted in once more.

"Yes and the freeloaders. We were making up for them with loud drinking, loud abuse and loud pigging out at the trough. That's when it all got messy."

The tape finished. "Find something else will you? Maybe some Deadboys?"

Cindy pulled the tape out, threw it in the back.

"Hey steady on, treat them with some respect, that's my only copy of that."

She looked over her shoulder. There were six or seven tapes already lying on the back seat. "When in Rome I always say." She opened the glove box again. There were two tapes left. "Hi-5 or Tom Waits?"

"Better make it Tom. We'll save Hi-5 for a more romantic moment."

Cindy turned the tape over in her hand. "Do you listen to this?"

He blushed. "It reminds me of Hank. I can't say I play it but I like having it with me."

Cindy watched him, loving the redness in his cheeks. He looked like such a kid sometimes. "Well maybe we'll play it on this trip." She put it back in the glove box. "Okay, on with the story. I want to hear about the food fight."

"Okay, okay. We were at the buffet and I said to Cass. "You know this free beer isn't going to last long, we'd better start getting two at a time."

He looked at me, double dipped in the cheese and chives and said, "Why not three?" "Hey, we don't want to be greedy." I turned to the bar. "You go that end, I'll do this end."

That was when Mark came over. "That guy doesn't know a damn thing about music. He thinks Nirvana started grunge. How did he get to write a book?"

He picked up a bowl of chips and wandered off.

"Should we tell Mark about the beer?" I asked Cass.

"I don't think he needs it. He's pretty happy without right now." Cassidy double dipped again. "I just wish he'd tell me the name of his shrink. He's on a good thing there."

We headed back to the bar."

"Did you ever find out the name of his shrink?"

Jason paused, looked over at her then back at the road. It spooled out in front of him, flat and continuous. He was glad to be talking. It kept him sharp.

"Is that relevant?"

"I don't know. Is it?" She was toying with him now. He felt his heart tearing slowly. He knew this moment would never be repeated. He felt a strange nostalgia soaking into him. He wanted to remember everything about this trip, every little movement she made, every sentence, every sound.

She must have sensed it. "Don't get soppy on me now old man. Just finish the story."

He wiped his eyes. "You want the story?"

She nodded. "I want the story. I want to know what you were doing when I wasn't around. I want to know what happened in your life. I never paid any attention before, we were too busy having fun or fighting."

He nodded agreement. "We were weren't we? Could have done with more fun and less fighting near the end though."

"Well, now's your chance," she said primly, "on with the tale."

He adjusted himself in the seat, squirming to get comfortable again. Long drives always hurt his back and legs. "Okay then. When the first band finally started we'd been to the bar many, many times."

"Surprise, surprise," she giggled.

He ignored her. "We stood at the front of the stage with Mark, eating chips and watching the bass player. She was young, blonde and dressed all in black. Cassidy was in love.

"She's gorgeous. Do you think she'd play in my band?"

Mark laughed at him. "You don't have a band Cass… just a guitar. And you haven't touched that in weeks. If playing with your dick counted though you'd be Jimi Hendrix."

Cassidy shrugged. "Hey, I can play as good as these guys, I just need the right band."

Mark was still laughing. "Or mittens." He dropped the chip bowl then and doubled over with laughter. "Just get some mittens mate, that's what you need."

We both looked at him.

"Fuck I wish I knew who his shrink was," said Cass then he went back to staring at the bass player."

"The bass player," said Cindy quietly, "Amy?"

"Yeah," Jason nodded, "Amy."

"I never really apologized to her."

"She'll live." He winced at the words. "Sorry."

He continued quickly with the story trying to keep the moment cheerful.

"The food fight started during the second band. Mark started it. He noticed Cassidy double dipping and confronted him.

"That's disgusting Cassidy. Other people have to eat this stuff you know."

Mark stuck his fingers in the dip and pulling them out, licked each one clean.

Cassidy did the same. "You are so right Mark. I don't know what I was thinking."

What was left of the literary crew shifted away. Mark scooped up a handful of salmon pate and offered it to Cass.

"Thank you Mark, I don't mind if I do," he said and then licked it from his palm.

That was when Jimmy Lancaster came over. "Excuse me fellas…"

Mark turned and said, "Jimmy my friend. Would you like some pate?"

Lancaster went pale. "No, I don't think so. Umm… do you think… do you think you could leave now?"

Cassidy looked hurt. "Leave? But we've only just got here. Besides we haven't really hurt anyone have we? I mean nobody was eating anyway, were they?"

He looked at Mark. "And it's not like we were having a food fight or anything…"

I tell you Mark took his cue beautifully. He smeared Lancaster's shirt with the Salmon pate and said, "Here have some Jimmy."

Lancaster looked down, blinked and then smiled. "Okay, if that's the way you want it."

He took us all by surprise. He poured his beer over Mark's shiny dome and then smeared an open mouthed Cassidy with sweet chili sauce. That was it, the food fight was on."

Cindy laughed. "You've kept yourself out of that mess well. Did you get involved?"

"We all did. Even the band had food thrown at it. Cassidy lost his job that night."

She put her hand on his leg, resting it gently. Jason liked the feeling. "What happened then?"

"Well, we lost Cassidy. We were standing outside the pub in these promo shirts that Jimmy had provided and I asked Mark, "Where's Cassidy then?"

"I dunno. He wandered off to talk to that bass player after the food fight.

That was the last I saw of him."

We were waiting for a taxi but none would stop.

Then a car pulled up. Two guys in suits stepped out. Plain-clothes cops, if a suit and a no. 2 cut can be called plain clothes. You ever noticed that? No one wears suits on a Saturday night except bouncers and wedding parties, and yet the cops always think they can mingle by wearing a suit?"

"I can't say I've paid attention," Cindy laughed, "but then my run-ins were always with uniformed cops."

"Well obviously I get in trouble at a better class of establishment."

Jason paused, wet his lips. "Shall I continue? You're not bored yet?"

Cindy faked a yawn. "Well, I'm hoping it gets better."

"Funny girl. Anyway, one of the cops, his hand twitching at his side asked, "You fellows okay?"

"Yeah, just waiting for a taxi, we just came from a book launch. Titanium Trousers…"

The other cop interrupted. "Book launch huh? You know a guy named Cassidy Hotchner?"

"Yeah. He was with us earlier." Mark looked at the cop. "Why?"

Both cops were smiling. "We just dropped him off at the city watch house. Obscene behaviour."

I had to ask. "What did he do?"

The twitchy cop looked at me. "Defecating in the street."

Then Mark burst out laughing. "He took a dump! Where was he?"

"In the mall as it happens. I don't see the humour in it myself," said Twitchy.

At least it wasn't at McDonalds though. Remember when Josh had been nearly arrested for indecent exposure. He'd walked into a McDonalds, ordered a Big Mac and when they handed it over said, "That's not a quarter pounder but this is." and unzipped. Hell, it even had cheese."

"I remember that," Cindy said. "I always thought he was exaggerating a bit but that changed my mind."

"You shouldn't have been so close."

"You didn't have to be," grimaced Cindy, "after that he was always waving it about."

"Well that night we weren't planning any public displays just waiting for a taxi.

It was time to get Mark home, the pills were wearing off and he was looking like joining Cass so I grabbed his arm. "We'll walk. We'll be okay. Keep up the good work."

"Yeah and watch where you're walkin' fellas."

That was when Mark said, "I wonder what happened to the girl then? She was pretty good on that bass you know…"

I told him, "Forget it. She wouldn't touch your instrument."

"How do you know?"

"I saw her at the Duke last Wednesday. Her name's Amy and she's got a girlfriend."

We crossed the street. There was a taxi rank.

"Hell, you could have told Cass that," he said.

We hopped into the first taxi.

"I reckon he knows by now."

Then we went back to the flat, drank bourbon, watched a Chuck Norris movie and passed out."

Cindy ran a hand through her scalp and tentatively said, "So that was where Amy first came into the picture. I had wondered."

"I thought you might have asked her yourself," Jason mumbled, "you did sleep with her." He instantly regretted saying that. The mood was gone now, Cindy looked tired again and Jason felt stupid, like he'd ruined everything even though he knew that wasn't strictly true. Fuck it, he thought, why can't you take words back? Why can't you rewind life like you can those shitty Chuck Norris movies?

"We didn't talk about that much. Or maybe I wasn't listening." Cindy shrunk into the corner of the seat. She stared out the window, still seeing her dream self standing over Jason, wondering just what it was she was looking for. The story was supposed to lighten the mood but yet again she hadn't been able to let go, to forgive him. And he hadn't even mentioned Nancy, she hadn't even been there then.

They traveled in silence and once again Jason wondered what answer he could give her, what he could say to make things right. If only it was that simple, if only there was a sentence, a string of words that would make it all make sense but he knew there wasn't. Their relationship was both too simple and yet strangely too complicated for anything to be easy.

Nancy, it all came down to Nancy. What was it about this one girl that made Cindy so mad? They had both had other relationships; they'd both sort of cheated on each other early on when neither would admit to any sort of bond other than sexual. So why did this one still raise her shackles?

Ten

It had been a Friday night. The Prince Henry had cheap drinks from 8 till 9 p.m. on Fridays. Starting at 10c a plastic cup of house draught, doubling in price every ten minutes, a limit of three drinks at a time. With practiced ease, Cassidy, Mark, Josh and Jason filled their table with cups and proceeded to drink mercilessly. At ten to nine some guy walked past and bumped the table. He spilt eight cups of beer, roughly fifty five or sixty cents worth. Mark stood up and head-butted him. When the bouncer came over, Mark head-butted him too. Mark had apparently forgotten to take his medication. Before they knew it, another eighty cents worth had been spilt, Josh had decked two more guys and they'd been thrown out. Cass kicked another bouncer in the nuts on the way out. Nancy was coming in as they were being escorted off the premises. Jason had seen her in the bookshop a couple of times when he was hanging around with Cass but hadn't really ever talked to her.

He called out over my shoulder. "Hi. Sorry, gotta go," as they pushed him out the door.

She laughed, turned around and followed them out. They went to the Duke and continued drinking. She surprised Jason by holding her own, she didn't look big enough to drink that much. Then it was back to Cassidy's for a party. By then there were about a dozen of them. Mark had calmed down by then and soon fell asleep in the love seat. Nancy and Jason casually migrated to his room and shut the door. The party continued on without them. It finished when Cassidy threw a deck chair off the balcony into the street below. They slept through it.

Jason bumped into Cassidy outside the record shop.

"Haven't seen you for a fair while Jason. Where you been?" He grinned at Mark.

"Just out Cass. Nothin' much," Jason shrugged, "been busy I guess."

He smirked. "Pussy whipped you mean. You're like a kid with his first root."

Jason hit him hard in the face and then kneed him in the groin. He went down.

"When you get your first root Cass I might listen to you."

Then he looked at Mark. He had his hands up.

"Hey, it's okay Jase. He deserved that one."

He helped Cassidy stand up. "Now how about a beer? All this fighting gives a man a thirst."

Jason laughed. "Why not? I've missed you dumb fucks. You're not as pretty but you're almost as much fun."

They sat at the bar while the boys filled him in on the news.

"No. 2 is vacant now," said Mark.

"Yeah? What happened? O.D.?"

"Nah," said Cass. "She got busted."

"Yeah," laughed Mark. "Got an honest cop who didn't want a blowie."

"Well he missed out," said Cassidy. "She was pretty good with those tonsils."

They both looked at him.

"Hey, she was having trouble getting her rent money together."

Mark looked disgusted. "Christ mate, I hope you went to the doctor. Who knows where that mouth has been?"

"So what have you got planned for the weekend?" Jason asked.

"Thought you'd be too busy," said Mark with a wry smile.

"Nancy's going to see her mum. She'll be away for the weekend." He blushed a little.

Cassidy smirked. "Oh. So you'll come out and play with us again huh? Well we might not want you to come over."

Mark continued. "Yeah, we might have some new kids to play with now."

"Right. Who else will play with you dropkicks anyway?"

"You would be surprised mate," grinned Mark. "We haven't been sitting around on our hands waiting for you."

"No we haven't," said Cass. "Our hands have been very busy."

"I'm sure of that Cass."

The boys had been busy. The mattresses were gone, the coffee table cleaned off, the records put away, there was even fresh milk in the fridge.

"What's happened here?" Jason stared at the freshly vacuumed carpet. "Is your mum coming to visit Cass?"

"Got a new flat mate," was all he said.

Amy then walked out of the bathroom, wrapped in a towel. "Hi Jason."

She walked into Mark's room and shut the door.

The boys stood there grinning.

Mark whispered in Jason's ear, "She plays more than one instrument."

The first hint of the trouble to come was from Al, the bartender at The Duke.

"You with Cindy tonight Jason?"

"Cindy? No, we've split up." He didn't like using those words but it was easier than trying to explain the complications he had got himself into. Cindy had come back from Queensland, seemingly ready to move back in with Jason, but Jason was seeing Nancy, was out partying, he didn't want to even try and settle down right now. He hadn't told her about Nancy, just said that he needed some time to readjust, that he was still trying to blow off steam after all the fighting and stress. They'd come to a loose arrangement about Hank. She was the main carer, he was the blow in who occasionally remembered to baby sit his son, Cindy dropping him at the shop, usually with chicken nuggets and fries in hand. They'd split up, he just hadn't got around to telling her.

He put Jason's beer on the bar. "Well be careful then. She's getting crazy. Last week she decked a bloke at the Arms with a pool cue."

Jason flinched. He'd heard about that already. Cindy didn't seem to get out much now, and he knew that was his fault, but when she did, things seemed to happen. And not all of them were good. The fun and frivolity had been replaced by something darker. He wondered how much of that was because they were apart, whether he was to blame for her violent moods. He was here though just to have a few drinks with Mark and Amy, he wasn't here to sort out his problems with Cindy. He was still basically in denial about his role in any of those problems.

There was a band in the back room so they went through to watch. Cindy was standing in front of them dancing, she was holding two drinks, one in each hand.

Mark nudged Jason. "So, you still interested in Cindy?"

"Shit, I don't know."

She looked good, all leg and sway and rhythm.

"You'd be mad not to be."

He watched her move and realised that yes, he would be mad not be.

She turned, saw him and smiled then moved up closer to the band.

Mark nudged him. "So I guess you are still interested?"

"I guess I am mate but it's more complicated than that. I'm seeing Nancy, there's Hank, there's this lifestyle we lead…"

"This is a lifestyle?" Mark slapped himself in the face. "Oh my gosh, I'm leading a lifestyle now. How long before it gets co-opted and sold as a reality show?"

"Give me a break. For the first time ever I give you a serious answer and what do I get? A public TV comedy skit." Jason finished his beer. "Want another?"

"Only if it fits in to your lifestyle mate."

He was back at the bar when Cindy appeared in front of him. He saw her hand coming up but was too slow. She slapped him across the face.

"You bastard!"

He was dumbfounded. "What the hell was that for?"

"I don't like men who cheat. My father did that." She poked him in the chest. "You're just like him."

He stood there rubbing his cheek, too drunk to really understand what was going on. "Your father? What?"

Jason stared at her wondering what to do. He and Cindy had always seen other people before the pregnancy. Hell, he was going out with someone else when they first went to bed together. "What has your father got to do with us?"

"He broke my mother's heart that bastard." She was starting to cry. "You're not doing that to me."

Al was behind Jason. "I told you," he whispered.

He was too slow again. Slap.

"Christ, will you calm down? I'm not your father."

He grabbed her arm. She bit him on the hand, breaking the skin. "Ow shit! Calm down Cindy."

"Bastard!"

"Will you calm down Cindy? I don't know what you're talking about."

She spat at him. "Nancy you prick. You've got yourself a girlfriend, cheating bastard. Does she know about me? Does she know about Hank?"

He looked over her head. Mark and Amy stood watching. Mark shrugged.

Cindy was looking at Jason. There was fire in those eyes. "Well?"

"Okay, so I've been seeing Nancy. I didn't realise it was such a big deal." He tried to look calm but he wasn't sure what was going on really. "It's nothing serious, you were gone, we kind of got together… but it's nothing serious, I would have told you."

He kept an eye on her hands this time.

"You're a man. Of course it's not serious."

Jason touched her arm. "Look Cindy, can we talk about this later?"

She smiled, her voice suddenly calmer. "I'm sorry. I guess I overreacted."

Jason relaxed.

She kneed him in the groin.

"You'll be okay. It's nothing serious."

She walked out.

Gingerly, using the bar as leverage, he pulled himself up.

Al stood on the other side of the bar grinning. "I did warn you Jase. Beer?"

He was sitting on the balcony with Mark. The sun was shining, the stereo was turned up and they had a bottle of Wild Turkey.

"Did I ever tell you my theory about Sesame Street?" asked Mark as he poured another drink.

"No I don't believe you've shared that theory with me as yet."

Jason sipped at the drink. Mark always made them strong.

"Well, I've been thinking about attention spans. How everyone's is shorter now."

He nodded, took another sip.

"And I reckon it's because of Sesame Street."

"I don't understand. How does Kermit the Frog give us a shorter attention span?"

Mark stood up and waved his arms. "Think about it. Sesame Street is, what, twenty or thirty years old now?"

Jason thought back. "Yeah, I guess so. I saw it when I was a kid, so that's gotta be twenty, twenty five at least."

"And what does the show do? It jumps from segment to segment…"

He paused as Amy came out in a t-shirt and tiny black shorts.

"Don't let me stop you," she said and rested against the balcony.

Mark continued. "You see, the show is short, sharp bursts of letters, numbers, songs… always changing styles and shapes, jumping around from segment to segment," He took another sip. "And it's been doing that for maybe thirty years and that's what… three or four generations of kids?"

"You're telling the story," Jason said.

"It's the same thing Jase. No attention span. Sound bites, media blurbs, cut and paste, Sesame Street. It's that show. We grew up on short bursts of letters and words and hand puppets and information and now we have no fucking attention span!"

He turned to Amy. "Do we?"

"Sorry," she said, "I wasn't listening."

Amy may have played more than one instrument but she was getting tired of tooting on Mark's flute. Her outfits were getting smaller and Cassidy's stares longer. The air dripped with sex and violence. Jason tried to stay away from it all. Nancy helped by refusing to go to the flat anyway.

"It's not them or me Jason. I know you need to see them, to play with the boys… but I'm not going to be there when you play, that's all."

With Nancy it was bookshops and art galleries, window shopping at Op shops and hitting the markets for books and old records. They'd go down to the port and have fish and chips and watch the boats docking. It was fun and he liked it but then he'd feel the need to 'dumb out', to not have to think or watch his words. He'd want beer, loud rock and the insanity that Mark and Cassidy provided without even trying.

Nancy would just shrug and say, "Have fun and be careful." As if you could do both at the same time.

The flat was in a mess. That was the first thing he noticed. There were pizza boxes on the floor, a trail of beer cans down the corridor and a solid lump of milk curd in the fridge. In the lounge lay five mattresses. Amy had left the building.

Cassidy was sitting on the balcony with a playboy magazine and a six pack.

"Hey stranger," he said. "Long time no drink."

"So it's back to two," Jason said as he pulled up a deckchair.

Cass handed him a lukewarm beer. "Yep. She fucked us up and then we fucked her off."

Jason could see the remnants of a black eye, just a slight bruising around the bags.

"So where's Mark?"

"He's seeing his shrink. He needs more happy pills."

"I can see that," Jason grinned. "So, you going to tell me what happened?"

Cass looked at him. Then he grinned back. "Okay so I fucked her."

He shrugged. "Who could resist that?"

"I take it Mark wasn't impressed?"

He opened another beer, flicking the cap over the balcony. "I think he expected it. He still hit me though, the prick."

There was silence while they both drank and Jason tried to imagine the scene. Mark could fight. He'd lost count of the fights he'd seen him in. They'd met Cassidy out the back of the pub when Mark was pounding on one of his friends. Cassidy was already big then, maybe nineteen years old and over six-foot tall. He could have stepped in to help his mate but he didn't. If you picked the fight, you fought it. Mark liked his style and soon the three were best of friends. Nothing had come between them. Jason wondered now if Amy finally had.

"So what about you? Are you and Mark still friends? Did you hit him back?"

Cass grinned again. "Of course I hit him back. I'm no soft cock."

"Who won?"

"We called it a draw. I got the black eye, he got the split lip." He stopped and scratched his groin. "We both got crabs."

Jason had to ask. "So where's Amy now?"

"You wouldn't believe me if I told you," laughed Cassidy.

Mark appeared in the doorway. He was smiling. He had his happy pills and a fresh six pack. "Go on tell him Cass." He was laughing now too.

"Apparently she's taken up with Cindy." Cassidy fell off his chair with laughter.

Jason couldn't help himself, he burst out laughing. Life just kept getting weirder.

Mark threw him a fresh beer. "Now that's an instrument that'll need a lot of practice."

Eleven

Cindy stared out the window but she wasn't seeing the scenery, the landscape instead she was seeing Amy. That petite frame, lean and tanned, her blonde hair, those blue eyes it was no wonder the boys fell for her, the girls too. Cindy had never really looked at a girl like that until she met Amy. This girl just exuded confidence, sex appeal, she knew that she had the looks that could turn heads. And yet she never really pushed it, never really took advantage of those looks, well not until she moved into the flat.

Cindy asked her one night why she had slept with Cassidy.

"I wanted to test them I think, to see just how strong their friendship was." She sat up and looked at Cindy. "It's silly but they sometimes seemed like they were the lovers you know?"

Cindy nodded. "I know. I think all boys are like that."

"Yeah, I guess so. But these guys I don't know… they really doted on each other. They wanted each other's approval for everything they did. Anyway, I didn't really love Mark or anything… it was sex that's all. And the excitement, the parties…"

She stroked Cindy's upper arm watching the goose bumps forming. "I like the excitement."

Cindy slowly ran her hand over Amy's uncovered leg. "I had noticed that."

She felt Amy's fingers traveling across her chest. "What about Jason?"

Amy stopped her travels. "No, he's with Nancy. That's different you know? Cass and Mark weren't with anyone else." Not for the first time she wondered just what Cindy was doing here in her bed, in her life. There was something there, some other motive. Cindy was the first person Amy hadn't really been able to read, she wasn't quite sure what this girl wanted. But Jason seemed to be the main focus. Amy knew about the boy, Henry or Hank or something but as far as she knew Jason and Cindy had stopped being a couple a long time ago. Cindy's fingers were tracing little circles on her upper thigh.

"So he wasn't tested?" her voice was quieter now.

"No," Amy said quickly, "he's a friend that's all. He's a funny guy and all that but he's just a friend." She withdrew her hand. "And like I said, he's with Nancy."

She felt Cindy's nails digging into her thigh. "Hey, that hurts."

Cindy's eyes were dark. "Don't mention that bitch again."

Amy pulled herself away. "Cindy, relax okay? I won't mention her."

She put her hand on Cindy's. "I'm sorry, I didn't realise how you felt."

Cindy looked down at her hand, noting the smooth skin, the tiny blonde hairs on her wrist and felt a twinge of anger. Had she touched Jason with those hands?

"I don't like her. She's a fake, a bitch, she thinks she's better than me but she's not."

Amy stroked Cindy's hand trying to calm her. "You haven't got over him have you?"

Cindy glared. "Got over him? Fuck him! And fuck her too!" She tugged her hand away.

"Don't you start defending that bastard. It's all right for him, fucking around and partying and shit. What about his son? What about Hank?"

Amy stood up quickly, grabbing her shirt and pulling it on. She was scared. She hadn't seen Cindy fire up like this before. She didn't know what to do, her powers didn't extend to this sort of confrontation. She could handle the boys and their whims, their macho showing off but this... this scared her.

"Maybe I should go home."

Cindy nodded, "Maybe you should."

Cindy rested her cheek against the car window. She had never really said sorry to Amy. But then Amy could look after herself. She smiled to herself, she'd proved that when they'd had the fight, the big one on New Years Eve. When Cindy had found out about the party, the fact that Amy's band were playing, that Jason would be there with that bitch, that Cindy wasn't invited… that was the fire that blew it all to the shithouse. Cindy couldn't remember much of it now, much of that period was a blur, just the feeling of abandonment, of pain, still surfaced occasionally but the moment by moment – a lot of that was just a flash, a blur of drinking and yelling and survival. But she did wish she had said sorry. It wasn't Amy's fault, she just happened to step into the firing line. Nancy got off lightly really. They all did. Cindy looked at her hands, so thin, almost transparent, they all got off lightly she thought but there was no bitterness. It was just a fact, just a fact.

On New Year's Eve the boys decided to throw a big party. It would involve all the flats and would happen in the backyard come car park. Amy's band was going to play. No. 2 was still vacant so the mattresses were dragged down to make it a crash pad. There was still a fridge in there too so the boys wiped it down, plugged it in and they had a beer fridge. Extension cords snaked out from the laundry for the lights, amps and stereo. Jason knew a few of the occupants in the other flats – the three metal heads in No. 1, the two girls who lived in No. 5, rock groupies both and had passed the odd nod or hello on passing but he didn't know the others. There was a gay bricklayer, Brad, in No. 3 and an Asian couple in No. 4 who showed their faces for a brief moment and then went back up the stairs very quickly. Jason guessed a brickie in a pink mesh top and a pair of stubbies wasn't a common sight back home. The three metal heads, Larry, Curly and Moe, had a litre bottle of tequila and designs on the groupies from No. 5. They had the right look, tattoos, long hair, unwashed and dazed, they just didn't play in a band. It was going to take a lot of work and most of the tequila to get the girls interested. Looking at the girls closely Jason wasn't sure if it was worth that much effort but then Larry, Curly and Moe were no prizes themselves.

Word had got around and there was soon a fair crowd in the backyard, maybe forty or fifty folk drinking, smoking and waiting for the band to start. The band was waiting for Amy. She showed up an hour late with bite marks on her arm and scratches down one cheek.

"I could have told you she was crazy," Jason said as he handed her a medicinal bourbon.

"Yeah?" she smiled. "You haven't seen what she looks like."

Nancy had come along but only lasted until 10-30.

"I'm going home Jason. It's too much for me, too loud, too many strangers."

He knew she wouldn't stay late but he had hoped she'd make it to midnight.

"Can't you stay till 12?"

She shook her head. "I'm sorry Jason. It's just not my thing. You stay though, call me in the morning."

Jason walked her to her car, kissed her. "Are you sure you can't stay just a little longer?"

"No, I'm uncomfortable here. I just want to go home and sleep."

He nodded. "Okay, I won't push you. I'll see you in the morning."

She wound down her window. "Be careful okay?" Then she drove off.

Jason walked back in to the yard to see Cindy screaming at Amy who was on stage playing. Cindy had a fat lip, scratches down both cheeks and a bandage wrapped around her hand.

She was chanting over and over, "You're going home in the back of an ambulance!"

Amy just smiled and kept playing. There was an empty circle around Cindy. Jason froze, not wanting her to see him, glad that at least Nancy wasn't here to witness this. He felt something, maybe sympathy welling up in him but he didn't know what to do.

No one seemed to know what to do. Then Mark stepped forward and offered her a drink. She took the cup, drank it straight down, spilling bourbon down her chin, and then threw the cup at Amy. It bounced off the speaker box. The band kept playing. Mark offered Cindy another drink. She did it all again. This time the cup hit the singer. Mark smiled, offered another drink. The cup hit the front of the stage. Another drink. Mark was mixing them stronger each time. Cindy was unsteady now, the cup slewed off to the right, missing the stage altogether. Mark took her arm and led her away. She followed meekly. Five minutes later he reappeared alone. Jason walked over.

"So what did you do with her?"

"She's asleep." He seemed embarrassed. "I couldn't let her go on, she'd have hurt herself."

"Will she be okay up there?" Jason could just see her trashing the flat if she woke up and was still angry.

"Don't worry I gave her some of my tablets. She'll sleep like a baby."

Jason was blushing, "I'm sorry man, I should have been the one to look after her…"

"It's okay mate, you aren't together anymore remember?"

Jason nodded. "I know." But inside he wasn't so sure that he did know. If he'd seen her with someone how would he react? He wondered if it wouldn't be him with the scratches, the bruises, the pain? He dropped his empty can on the ground. "Beer?"

They went to the fridge in No. 2. It was empty.

"Shit. Where's it all gone?" Mark looked at Jason. "What's the time?"

"Elevenish I think."

"Good. We've still got time for a beer run. Let's get some money out of these pigs."

Jason ended up in charge of the beer run.

"Why me?"

"We trust you," said Cassidy. "You'll keep an eye on Mark, make sure we get beer and not fucking Kahlua or Curacao."

Mark had once gone out with everyone's hard scavenged money and decided on the way that the boys should make cocktails. Instead of coming back with two cartons of VB, he came back with various coloured liqueurs and two girls named Tammy and Sammi. The girls were welcome, but not the 'shampoo & conditioner' as Cassidy referred to anything that wasn't amber coloured.

After finding a near sober driver they went to the Duke. It was packed. Al was behind the bar.

"Al, I need some takeaways. We've run out."

He laughed. "Not from here Jase. We've got fuck all ourselves. John's out trying to buy some for us now."

"Shit. Okay we'll try the Prince."

The Prince Henry had beer. They tried to charge close to twice the normal price being a 'special night and everything'. The boys left with a fuck you, no supplies and two bouncers hot on their trails. At five to twelve they found a bottle shop in the throes of closing.

"Stop, stop!" shouted Mark out the car window as the sliding door was coming down.

The door stopped. A youngish guy peered under it.

"We have money! We need beer!"

He hauled the door back up. Jason climbed out of the car.

"Three cartons of VB and a bottle of Rebel." he said.

Mark pulled out another twenty. "Better make that two bottles of Rebel. This is thirsty work."

They arrived back at the flats to be hailed as conquering heroes. Jason raised his arms in victory and promptly dropped a bottle of bourbon. Luckily it bounced and they were still heroes.

Amy came over. "You missed midnight Jase."

"Shit, we did too."

She kissed him on the cheek. "Happy New Year."

Jason woke up on a mattress in No. 2. The sun was streaming through the window, his head felt like Tyson was pounding some poor bastard from side to side and his mouth felt like a sandpapered toilet bowl. Curled up on the mattress with him was Amy.

She opened her eyes. "Morning, how do you feel?"

"Like shit."

She smiled "I'm not surprised. You and Mark really hammered that bourbon."

He stood up and stretched, feeling his back un-kink and straighten out. Amy sat up she looked good. Jason hated that about women. They always woke up looking good, fresh. He always woke up, feeling and looking like he had slept in a vat of shit.

He had to ask. "Did we… did we do… anything?"

A laugh. "No, we just talked and then you fell asleep. You looked so lonely, I stayed with you." She shrugged. "I guess I fell asleep too."

"Shall we go up and wake the boys? I could do with a coffee and a piss. Not necessarily in that order though."

Amy hesitated. "Cindy might still be there."

"I hadn't thought of that."

Amy stood up, stretched. She did it with much more style than Jason had. "My place is just up the road."

It was Jason's turn to hesitate.

She smiled. "I don't bite. Well, not straight away."

"Sorry," he said trying to sound casual. "It's not you, I'm just… well…"

"Attached? Maybe still thinking about Cindy?" She was still smiling. She ran a finger down his cheek. "Don't worry, I'm off men right now. Women too I think."

She picked up her bass guitar and they walked out of the flat. The car park was awash with plastic cups, beer cans and broken glass. Curly and Moe were asleep on the stage. Larry was nowhere to be seen. Later on they found out he spent the night with Brad the bricklayer.

Amy pointed. "My car's over the road. Coming?"

Jason followed, not really knowing why but with that early morning feeling of still being slightly drunk, that feeling of not yet wanting to end the party.

After leaving Cassidy's, or getting kicked out, depending on who was telling the story, Amy had got a bed-sit on the edges of the city centre. She didn't have much, a bed, her bass guitar, a small dresser in one corner. Her clothes were still in a suitcase on the end of the bed. There was a deck chair folded against the wall. Jason looked for signs of Cindy but all he could see was a Christmas card.

"Take a seat, I'll get us a coffee."

She headed off to the kitchen. She came back holding two cups of steaming black coffee. "Sorry, some fucker's used all the milk again. At least there was still coffee."

Amy sat on the bed, Jason had the deck chair.

"So, what happened between you and Cindy?" he asked.

Amy looked away, giving him a good look at the scratches. "She's crazy," she said quietly.

"I know that. I copped it at the pub, remember?"

She turned back to him. "She still likes you. I mean really likes you."

He had to laugh. "Yeah? Funny way of showing it."

Amy blushed. "The fight was over you." She put her head down. "She thinks we slept together."

Jason didn't know what to say. He put his coffee down and watched Amy. Her cheeks were still pink. "She thinks that if I slept with Mark and Cass, well then I must have slept with you too."

"I hope you set her straight." It sounded meaner than it was supposed to. "Sorry, I didn't mean it that way."

"Of course I did. She's jealous though, she won't believe me." She sipped at her coffee. "She wouldn't let it go."

When she looked at Jason, he had to look away. He focused on the wall behind her shoulder. He could see the bubble and warp of salt damp hiding under the wallpaper.

"I don't get it though. How can she be jealous? She left town, took Hank with her. What was I supposed to do? Wait in case she did come back?"

Amy slid off the bed and stood in front of him. She still looked fresh. "I think maybe she expected you to. And you didn't and she doesn't know what to do about it."

"But then why did she…" he paused, searching for the right words, "take up… with you…"

Amy smiled. "We didn't really do anything. She just wanted to find out what you were doing I think. Maybe get you jealous. She's not into girls really."

Jason stood up. He was now face to face with Amy.

She kissed him on the cheek. "You'd better go or she might have a reason to beat me up."

This time Jason blushed.

"Where the hell have you been?"

Jason stopped in his tracks. He was sure Mark was still on his pills but he didn't sound or look like it right now. He was pacing the lounge, stepping over empty cans and CD covers. His face was tightly drawn. "I've been ringing your place all fucking morning!"

Jason made sure to keep his back to the nearest exit. "I was at Amy's. What's the matter?"

"Not much… just a fucking O.D. that's all. And then trespassing." He kept pacing. "We've had cops, ambulances, the landlord…"

He stopped in the middle of the room. Under his foot was a copy of Rolling Stone, the one with Kurt on the cover. "It's been a shit of a morning."

Jason relaxed a bit, stepped into the room. "What are you talking about? An O.D.? Who?"

"The mother of your child, that silly bloody bitch Cindy." He slumped into a deck chair. "She found the rest of my happy pills."

Jason sat down. "Shit. Is she okay?"

"Yeah but she spewed all over my bed."

Jason tried not to smile. "You weren't in it were you?"

Mark's face creased. He tried to suppress his grin. "No I fucking wasn't."

Jason sat in the chair trying to work out what he was feeling, whether the relief was because Cindy was okay or simply because he wasn't there when it happened. He wondered how he would have dealt with it, if he could have dealt with it.

He got up and headed towards the kitchen, calling back, "Got any beer?"

"Yeah, in the crisper. I hid them from Cassidy."

He found two cans in a brown mushroom bag.

"Where is the big boof anyway?" Jason asked as he came back into the lounge. He handed Mark a can.

"Thanks." Mark drank deeply. "He's with the landlord. We had new tenants move into No. 2 today."

"Fuck, what time was that?" Jason tried to remember what time he'd left.

"Jeez, I don't know. Just after the Ambos had taken Cindy away. Half tennish I guess."

They'd missed them by half an hour. "Was anyone still in there?"

"Coupla kids from up the street. But the place was a mess. Mattresses, empty bottles…" Mark dropped his empty can on the floor. "And someone had spewed in the bathroom. Wasn't you was it?"

Jason tried to recall if he'd vomited last night. "No I don't think so. I was pretty good for a change."

"First time for everything." Mark stood up. "Duke open today?"

"Yeah I think so. Why?" Jason finished his can, dropped it on the pile.

"All this savin' lives and talkin' to cops has got me thirsty, that's why." He headed towards the door. "Coming?"

He didn't need to ask again.

An hour later Cassidy showed up. "Thought I'd find you two here."

"How'd it go?" Jason asked as he signaled for another round.

"He was pissed off but I offered to clean up the mess and told him I didn't know who the squatters were or how the mattresses got there…" He waved his arms, "and he calmed down a bit then."

He picked his pint up and drank it down in one long gulp. "Oh… and he took our bond money."

Mark spilt his beer down his shirt. "Shit, can he do that?"

"I wasn't really in a position to negotiate too much," said Cass. "He was originally gonna call the cops in."

"Well he wouldn't have had to shout. They were upstairs grilling me about psycho-girl," replied Mark, wiping the beer of his front.

They both looked at Jason. "No more Cindy, okay Jase."

"Hey, what did I have to do with it?" he asked, as if he didn't know.

Cassidy put his arm around his shoulder. "For some reason, despite the fact that you are a well-known prick, uglier than a bag of rats on a stick and useless to boot, she still loves your scrawny little arse to death. I mean really, really loves your scrawny little arse."

Mark smiled. "And she saw you leaving with Amy this morning. That's why she took my fucking pills."

This time Jason spilt his drink.

Twelve

Jason decided that maybe it was time to keep a low profile. He didn't go out much at all except for work and he gave most of the hours to Josh anyway. No parties, no drinking at the flat, just work and home and occasionally, Nancy. One day Cindy showed up at the record shop. Hank wasn't with her, in fact Jason hadn't seen his son for a month. She didn't say a word, just browsed for hours. Or maybe it just seemed that long. Finally she came up to the counter.

"Hello Jason, how are you?" she asked, a small grin crossing her face.

He looked down at the counter, pretending to study a catalogue. "Fine, I guess."

"And how is Amy?" she asked.

"Amy? I really wouldn't know. Haven't seen her."

He looked up. The grin was gone, those dark eyes were burning again. "Liar!"

She stormed out of the shop.

Nancy rang him a few nights later.

"What have you been up to Jason?" she asked blandly.

"What do you mean?"

"I've had some very strange phone calls lately."

The neutrality was gone now. She was starting to sound pissed off.

"What? Obscene calls or something?" he asked, already dreading the answer.

"No, just strange." She paused and he heard her take a deep breath. "A girl keeps calling and whispering something."

"Whispering what exactly?"

"I don't really know. She talks too fast and too quiet." Another breath, "But it's about you Jason. I know that much. She says she's knows about us, knows about me… just what does she know Jason?"

He tried to think of a way to explain what was going on here.

"Nancy, it's nothing. It's Cindy. She wants me back."

"Uh huh."

He could tell he wasn't going to get any help here. "Look, she's gone kind of crazy. She thinks we're still an item, me and her I mean. She won't let go."

"Why would she think that Jason?" He could almost feel the ice coming down the phone line. "And why would she warn me to watch out for Amy?"

"She did what?"

"I think we should talk Jason, tomorrow when I've calmed down. I'll see you after work."

She hung up. He put the phone down, picked it straight back up, hesitated and then put it down again. She was right they didn't want to do this over the phone.

Nancy came into the shop just before closing. They went to Sam's for pizza.

"So why does Cindy still think there is something going on between you two?" Nancy asked as Jason poured them both a wine.

He drank his down quickly. "I don't know. She'd been gone for six months, as far as I knew it was all over." He poured himself another drink. "It was never really serious in the first place, you know?"

Her voice was flat. "You have a son together. That to me is serious."

"I meant Cindy and I, we were never meant to be serious. Sure Hank made it a bit more… I don't know, more of a relationship I guess but when she went to Queensland…" he shrugged and looked away, "I thought that was that, it was over, whatever it was."

Nancy looked him in the eye. "Have you slept with her since she came back?" Those light brown eyes darkened. "Or Amy?"

"No I haven't. Christ, I had a drink with her, that's it." He drank another glass. "She's the one who slept with Amy not me."

He took a deep breath. "Look, Amy, Mark and Cassidy have told me to watch out for her. She's still in love with me or some bullshit like that."

"Why though Jason? What did you do? This isn't normal behaviour."

The waiter arrived with the pizza. He ordered another carafe. He had the feeling he'd need it.

He turned back to Nancy. "I didn't do anything Nancy. You gotta believe me. I mean I saw her when she first came back, we worked out some arrangements for Hank but there was nothing else."

He picked up a slice of pizza, dropped it onto his plate. "Then we bumped into her at the Duke, she hit me and went home. I didn't see her again until New Years Eve."

"She hit you?" Nancy picked at her food. He really hated that. Why order pizza if you're going to pick bits off.

"Yeah, I should have realised then. She found out I had a girlfriend and started abusing me." He shrugged. "Next thing I know she's supposedly going out with Amy."

"Who you haven't slept with either?"

"No I fucking haven't." He was shouting.

The waiter stopped a couple of tables away. He had Jason's wine. Jason signaled to him. He brought the fresh carafe over.

Jason said quietly, "Look Nancy, I don't know what her problem is but I've done nothing to encourage her. I just didn't discourage her I guess. I don't want any problems with her, Christ she's got my son."

He poured himself a fresh glass and started eating. Nancy said nothing for a while, just picked at her pizza.

"How did she get my number?" she finally asked.

"I don't know. She's crazy not dumb. I really don't know."

It was time to leave. "Look, I'll talk to her try and explain. If she rings again just tell her you already know I'm a bastard."

Nancy nodded okay. As they left he looked at her plate, she'd left the best bits.

It was a fill in shift at The Duke. Al was sick and Jason wasn't planning anything, except beers at Cassidy's so when Al asked him if he could do it he said, 'sure I'll do it'.

Cindy walked in at five to nine. He knew the time because it was five minutes until his break. She sat at the bar. "Black Sambuca please."

Jason got her a drink then went to the other end of the bar. John came over, "Better make it a short break tonight Jase, looks like it could be busy."

He nodded, "Sure, I just want to grab a bit to eat. Ten minutes or so."

Cindy was sitting at the other end watching him. She raised her empty glass. He tapped John on the arm. "Get that will you? I'll just go grab something from the kitchen."

He barely made it to the kitchen before he heard raised voices. He came out to see John clutching his bleeding face and Cindy screaming at him. Other patrons had moved back warily. Jason thought about stepping back into the kitchen but Cindy saw him. She picked up her glass and threw it at him. It smashed behind him.

"You bastard! You left me alone with these pigs!"

He stepped forward slowly over the broken glass. "I was just getting something to eat Cindy. I'm here now."

He held his hands up defensively, just like the movies. "Just calm down and we'll have a drink okay?"

"You wouldn't even get my drink for me. You sent him!" She swung at John but he was well out of range now.

He took another step forward, hands still up. "I was just taking a break Cindy, that's all." He pointed to the clock. "See I have a break at nine." It was 9.05.

In a quiet voice she said, "You're back now?"

"Yes I am." Another step.

"You won't leave me alone?"

"No, I won't leave you alone."

He turned to John, "Two Sambucas John."

"One drink Jase and then you get her out of here okay?"

"Sure John." He guided Cindy to a seat. "You okay now?"

She murmured assurances and he got the drinks from the bar.

"Here, drink this and me and you will go somewhere else okay?"

She picked up her glass, filled her mouth with black and leaned towards him. They kissed, the burning liquor swirling around their tongues and mouths. Then she bit down hard. Jason pulled back, Sambuca spilling down his shirt. He could feel the blood in his mouth, coppery sweet, mingling with the remnants of the drink.

"What the fuck are you doing?"

She smiled. "You're mine again Jason. It's in our blood. Remember? The blood on the walls?"

He spat in his glass. "That was a different time Cindy, things change."

"No Jason, we're bonded by blood. We always will be."

He pushed back his chair. "Come on, it's time to take you home."

He took her hand and helped her stand.

"Back in a little while John."

John grinned, the scratches on his cheek red and raised. "Good luck."

Cindy seemed oblivious. She was licking her lips and smiling. They walked outside and Jason turned to her. "Come on Cindy, I'll take you home."

She shook her head. "I want to stay with you."

"I have to get back to work?"

He led her towards his car.

"No!" She stood there, arms crossed. "I'm not going."

Hands out again, he stepped closer. "Look, I've got to get back to work. You won't be allowed back in…"

She frowned. "But I want to stay with you."

He shook his head. "I'm going back to work. I can take you home or I can leave you out here." He thought of the damage she could inflict out here, the pub windows, his car. "Look, what if I take you around to Cassidy's? When I finish work, I'll come back there too. What about that?"

"Cassidy's? They don't like me. They'll call the police again."

It was almost like dealing with Hank he thought bitterly.

"No, they won't. You can listen to records with Cass and Mark and when I finish here, I'll come and get you." He guided her towards the car again.

"You promise?" Her dark eyes were shining again. The moonlight made her skin even paler. The high cheekbones, dark ringlets of hair cut short, this was the girl who had stolen his heart.

"I promise."

Jason woke up on a mattress, Cindy still asleep next to him. She looked peaceful now, childlike. A few hours before she'd thrown a full can of beer at him. Now she was smiling in her sleep, stirring only slightly as he carefully eased out from under the quilt and padded quietly into the kitchen. Cassidy sat at the table.

"Coffee?" he asked holding up a takeaway from the servo.

"It'll do for a start I guess." He took the cup, it was lukewarm. "Been awake long?"

Cass smiled. "I couldn't sleep mate, not with her in the place. I was too scared she'd knife us or something."

He wasn't joking. "Come on Cass. She's not that bad. She's not a killer, just a little…"

"Nuts? Homicidal? I know, psychotic."

He finished his coffee. "Seriously Jase, she is dangerous. I kept expecting to hear her screaming or you…" He shrugged, "so I sat up all night watching you sleep."

"You did what? Come on you're not serious?"

Cassidy was blushing. "I am, I did. I didn't trust her."

Jason looked at his cup it was empty. "Got anything stronger?"

Cass pulled a bourbon bottle from the cupboard. "There's a bit left."

They drank it straight.

"You've got to get her out of here Jase. And out of your life." He poured them both another. "She's dangerous mate, seriously dangerous."

Jason drank, listening to the sounds of the city stirring outside. "She's my ex Cass, she's the mother of my kid. Sure, she's a bit fucked up right now but then who isn't?"

The bottle was empty. "It's different with her Jase. Mark's a fuckup sure but I've never been scared of him, not really. She doesn't know when to stop though."

Jason thought back to the fight. He'd finished work at one, left John to clean up and come back to the flat. It was quiet. Mark and Cassidy were in the kitchen. In the lounge sat Cindy staring at the TV.

"She's been waiting for you Jase. Barely said a word to us."

He grabbed two beers and went into the lounge. She looked up and smiled. "You came back. I didn't think you would."

He sat next to her. "I told you I would." He handed her a can. "We'll have a drink and then I'll take you home."

Another smile. "I'd like that."

She turned back to the TV. Jason got up and looked out through the balcony doors. The neon sign at the service station wasn't working properly. The 'S' was out, it just said 'hell' now.

She said quietly, "I'm looking forward to seeing your new place."

He didn't turn. "No, I said I'd take you home, to your place."

He heard her move. Then the can exploded into the wall next to him. Beer splashed over Jason, the floor and glass. When he turned she was staring at the TV again.

He finished his beer and dragged a mattress in from the hallway. "We'll sleep here then."

She curled up in his arms and he stroked her head until she stopped crying and went to sleep. He lay there wondering what the hell he was doing. What had happened to her, to them? When she came back from Queensland she had been edgy, impatient, wanting to know where they stood, what he was going to do for Hank, for her. He'd told her he honestly didn't know. He had waited those first couple of months but when she hadn't come back he'd assumed it was all over, that that party was finished so he'd started another. He hadn't expected to see her or Hank ever again. He was surprised when she did come back, when she showed up in the shop one morning with his son smiling behind her. He wasn't ready for it, didn't know what to say or do. He was seeing Nancy but he didn't tell Cindy. He'd told her he needed some time, some space to work out what he was going to do. He wasn't sure he could be a father, a partner again, hell, he wasn't sure about anything. He just wanted to have fun. He knew it was selfish but that was just the way it was. At the time she seemed to take it well, now he wondered just what she was really thinking. Finally he fell asleep, one arm draped over her. If anyone else had looked in and not known what had just happened they would have assumed they were still a couple.

The sun was now shining through the kitchen window, bravely struggling with the dirt and mould of the windowpanes. Cass was sitting silently watching Jason.

"So what do I do then Cass?" He sipped the last of the bourbon. "I can't leave her here."

Cassidy shook his head. "She's not your problem Jase. You don't owe her. The past is the past." He stopped. "You haven't done anything recently, have you?"

Jason shook his head. "I'm just trying to stop her from hurting herself… and anyone else."

"Like Nancy?" he asked, "Does she know…" He trailed off, just pointed to the lounge room."

"Some of it, yeah." He just wanted to go home and get some more sleep, forget the whole night. "Cindy got her number." He looked at Cass.

"Shit, that was me. Sorry."

Jason was too tired to be angry. "Doesn't matter, she would have got it somewhere. She's very persistent."

He stood up, yawned. His bones creaked and cracked from the bad mattress. "Jeez I wish Mark would choose better mattresses. Look, when she wakes up I'll take her home."

Cassidy stood up too, picked up the empty bottle and looked at it almost longingly.

"Do you know where she lives now?"

"I've thought of that. I'll ring Amy."

"She's on tour. You'll have to think of something else."

He opened the bottle, tilted it back and sucked the last drops out.

The voice came from behind them, it was Cindy.

"You could always just ask me."

Cassidy dropped the bottle. It broke.

Nancy put the book back on the pile. They'd just been to a sale. There were two piles, the ones he would get around to reading eventually and the ones he might get around to reading eventually. He was going to need a new bookshelf. He thought it odd that now he had a record shop he rarely bought any music for himself. Instead it was books.

"I hear you had a bit of trouble at the Duke recently," Nancy said, picking another book up.

Jason tried to appear unconcerned. "Mm, just Cindy acting up. No big deal."

He shuffled through the piles. "Who told you?"

She flicked through the book. "No one you know. One of the girls from my class was there." She put the book down. "She said you were with Cindy."

"No I was working. Remember, I did that fill in for Al?"

He plucked a book from the second pile and put it on the first pile.

"You kissed Cindy."

Jason looked at her. She was very calm, still. No emotions showing at all. It was more frightening than Cindy's wild eyes.

"I was trying to get her to leave." He felt tired again. "I just wanted her out the door."

"So you kissed her?" Still no emotion.

"I thought it might calm her down. She was pretty freaked out." He had a book in his hand, just turning it over and over. "I just wanted her to go home."

"Did it work?" Her voice cracked. "Did she… go home?"

He looked at the cover, Bukowski – Women. "Eventually."

He put the book on the second pile; he'd already read it.

Later, lying in bed, Nancy asleep next to him Jason started thinking about madness. Cindy was definitely off the edge now. She'd always been a bit crazy he knew, he couldn't deny that that was part of his attraction to her but this was different, this was scarier. There'd always been an element of roughness, of violence in their sex play, a sort of domination game of mind and body but it had never been this intense, this violent. Sure he'd been jealous of some of the boys she'd taken home when they were first seeing each other but then he was seeing other people too, it hadn't seemed to matter that much. He'd never really had any serious problems with it, never really stalked her or raised a fuss. But then neither had she. What had happened to change her? Was it simply parenthood? Did something happen in Queensland? She said something about her father having affairs, had that pushed her over? Had he? Or was she always like this? Had he just not noticed while he was with her? Was he that selfish that he hadn't seen the signs?

But then he thought Nancy had some strange ideas too. She came from a strong Catholic background and hadn't even told her family about him yet. As far as they knew she was still a virgin, a good Catholic girl studying to better herself. And that Catholic guilt had carried over into the bed too. She wouldn't undress in front of Jason, the light had to be off or the shades drawn. And she always kept something on, her singlet usually or her shirt, occasionally even just one sock, one item of clothing so she wasn't completely naked. It didn't feel so sinful then she told him. And while she was prepared to go down on Jason, he wasn't allowed near her that was wrong, that was sinful. Madness just seemed a matter of degrees. Cindy made a public display of her craziness, Nancy's was more internal, guilt ridden and in the dark. And his? Hell, he wasn't even sure yet what his was.

Thirteen

The telephone was ringing. He woke groggily and thrashed around looking for it. Something fell, a glass then a book then he found the phone. It was Cassidy.

"This had better be fucking good Cass, its 2 a.m."

He sounded tired. "You'd better come over Jase. We have a little problem."

"What problem? What are you talking about?"

He already knew though.

"It's Cindy. She's here looking for you."

He pulled on a pair of jeans, found a jumper in the wash basket and got his boots. It felt like there was a huge weight pressing down on him. He was sure that he was walking with a stoop but when he looked into the mirror, he looked fine. Straight and tall, it was just his eyes that were weighed down. It was scary. His eyes were starting to get that dull sheen that he'd seen in Cindy's eyes when she was staring at the TV screen.

Mark met him at the door. The glass pane was broken. "She's in my room. Less to break in there."

Jason stepped over the shards of glass and into the hall. There was blood on the wall, a handprint. Mark saw him staring.

"She cut herself when she punched the glass out."

Drops of blood, tacky and brownish stained the carpet. "Is she okay?"

"Yeah, Cassidy got her to let him look at it."

"How?"

He shrugged. "He promised to call you."

Mark's bedroom door opened. Cassidy stepped out, signaled to Jason. He walked over. The weight was even heavier. He was sure he was stooped now.

"Is it safe?" he asked, feeling stupid even as the words left his mouth,

Cassidy just nodded. Jason went in, shutting the door behind him.

Cindy was sitting on the mattress. Her right hand was wrapped in a tea towel. She was crying. This wasn't how it was supposed to be, this wasn't how she had planned it. Where was he when she needed him? Where was he, with some other woman, some other slut. What about their relationship? What about Hank? She just wanted to make things right for Hank, she wanted her son to have a father, was that so wrong?

"I missed you Jason. Why didn't you call? You said you would call."

He sat next to her. "I guess I've been busy."

He pointed to her hand. "How's your hand? Does it hurt?"

She looked down at the tea towel. There was a red stain slowly showing through. "It's all right, it's just a cut."

She started to cry again. "They wouldn't let me in. I had to punch the glass Jason, they wouldn't let me in."

"Cindy," he paused. What could he say? "Cindy… this has to stop."

He stood up. "There's nothing between us anymore Cindy." He tapped his head. "It's all in your head and it has to stop."

Jason swore he saw the ignition flame. Her eyes fired and she stood up.

"You bastard! You're just like the rest, like my father… you're like all of them!"

She hit him hard in the face. The tea towel smelt old and damp. He wondered where the hell Cassidy found it anyway. He'd never seen one in the flat before. She hit him again. He just stood there. He didn't know what else to do. He could feel the blood trickling from his nose. She continued to hit him. He didn't know how many times she hit him but when she finally stopped his nose was gushing red and he could feel one eye closing.

"Are you finished?" he asked quietly.

She slumped back down onto the mattress. Strangely she felt calmer now, she had needed to hit him, to make him feel some of the pain she was feeling. She took a deep breath and relaxed. Fuck him and his self-righteous bullshit. Fuck his friends too. Fuck all of them. They had no idea what was going on, how she felt, how she had to cope with it all on her own. Their little boys club, this gang of drunken wankers, all laughs and beer and girls and ha ha isn't life fucking great. Well it wasn't fucking great, not by a long fucking shot. And he was as bad as the rest of them, so pious and innocent, with that nothing was his fault bullshit. She thought about hitting him again but she couldn't even raise the energy. She just wanted to sleep now, to have a rest and dream for a while.

Jason pulled a handkerchief from his pocket and tried to stem the flow from his nose.

"I'll take you to the hospital if you want. They can look at your hand."

She didn't say anything. He walked out, stood in the hall. Cindy followed soon after.

"She won't bother you anymore boys."

No one said anything. Jason walked her out to the car. At emergency he found her a nurse and left her there. She hadn't said a word. By the time he got home his left eye was swollen shut. He collapsed onto the bed. He wondered who was looking after Hank, maybe her cousin Greg. He thought briefly about ringing him but he fell asleep before he could find his number.

Jason called Josh and told him to look after the shop. He found Greg's number and told him what had happened. Greg said he sort of knew anyway. Cindy had come back from the hospital but Greg wouldn't let her have Hank.

"We'll look after him until you two sort things out."

Jason wondered what that meant. Did it mean he would end up with Hank? He couldn't imagine himself being able to do that, he couldn't see himself being a father, day in and day out. But then he'd expected Cindy to instantly become a mother hadn't he? He didn't want to think about the fact that he was probably at least partially to blame for Cindy's condition. So instead, he hid in the flat with his books and two litre bottles of vodka. He got an answering machine from his neighbour.

"Good price for you Jason, straight from the warehouse."

Jason didn't ask him how he broke into the warehouse.

Each morning he'd look in the mirror, see that dull right eye blinking back and pour a vodka to start the day. By the third day, the swelling had gone down and he could see the dullness in both eyes. He went out and bought another litre.

It was the maggots that broke the stupor. It was hot that week and the flat had become a sweatbox. Jason was sitting in the lounge listening to Chet Baker's doom laden croak when he saw them. There was a trail of wriggling white across the floor. He put his vodka aside and stood up. Next to his chair was a pile of take-away boxes, chips, chicken bones, pizza crusts. The maggots were coming from the rubbish bin in the kitchen to the collection of scraps in the lounge. One long line of glutinous, writhing fly larvae having a fine time in the house of pain. Jason looked around him. The coffee table was covered in books, dirty glasses and paper plates. The whole room stank of sweat and alcohol. It was sour, rancid and cloying. It was worse than Cassidy's. How could he have let it get this bad? He went to the kitchen, found a rag and started the clean up.

There were eight messages from Nancy, each shorter than the last. Finally she just said, "Call."

He called. "Hi, it's me. I'm back, I think."

There was a brief silence, "And I'm supposed to do what?"

Jason was stunned. "S-sorry, I just thought I should call you, tell you…"

"Tell me what? That you've come out of hiding?" She was shouting now, "that maybe you can fit me in between all your women, all your dramas!"

He recoiled from the phone, holding it away from his ear, waving the receiver in the air as if he could shake out her anger. Then he could hear laughter.

"You still there?" he asked gingerly.

"You egotistical prick. Ever think I might not want you back?"

"I couldn't blame you if you didn't. But I'm back anyway. Want to go somewhere and talk? I need some fresh air."

She laughed again but it wasn't a pleasant sound this time. 'Well that rules out Cassidy's."

"I'll come over and pick you up."

"And Cindy? Where does she stand?"

"She's the past. Let the past stay buried."

"Can you do that Jason? Can you honestly do that? I've been doing some thinking too and I don't know if this is the way I want to live my life."

He didn't know what to say. "Um, look I'll come and get you and we'll talk okay?"

He hung up before she could answer, grabbed his keys and stepped outside. He looked up at the sky. It was clear, bright, not a cloud to be seen. Jason took a deep breath. For the first time in a long time he didn't feel tired, he felt good and clean and alive. Then he heard her.

"Bastard!"

She came running towards him. He saw his car behind her, its windows smashed, the tires slashed, paint daubed all over it. In her hands she had a baseball bat. He remembered it was a present for Hank then she swung wildly and Jason was down on his knees clutching his chest, gasping for breath. He saw stars, literally. It was like being in a Tom & Jerry cartoon, little lights flashing around his head but he swore they were there.

He woke up on his bed. Cindy was sitting on the end of the bed, legs folded, reading Women. "You know, I preferred Post Office. This one is just him bragging about all the girls he's scored with." She put the book down. "Are all men like that?"

Jason groaned and tried to sit up but his back screamed in pain so he lay back down on the pillow. Cindy crawled up and lay next to him. "We need to talk Jason."

He nodded. His mouth was dry and he was still feeling woozy. He couldn't see the bat anywhere but he was scared that she still might have it close by. "Okay," he croaked.

"I'm sorry I hit you but you just get me so frustrated sometimes." She stroked his brow.

"Hank wants his dad back."

"And you?" He licked his lip, felt the flecks of dried blood. "Do you want his dad back?"

She cocked her head a little and he instantly pictured an eagle eyeing off its prey. "Maybe. When I went to Queensland I didn't really think about it or you. But when I came back… well, maybe I did miss you a little." She sat up and jumped off the bed.

"But when I got here you didn't seem to have missed me. You were too busy playing with the boys." She was fiddling with something on the floor. He tried to look over the side of the bed but shards of pain ran through his neck and back as soon as he moved.

"And there were those girls of course. The sluts you were fucking."

"Cindy…"

She showed him what she was holding. In one hand she had a lighter, in the other a can of lighter fluid. "I was going to set this place on fire… but I changed my mind."

She flicked the lighter, watching the flame. "I decided that Hank needs his dad more than I need to punish him." She threw the lighter on the bed. "Even if his dad is just another cheating prick like his grandfather."

Jason shifted his weight, trying to ease the stabbing pain in his neck. "What is this about your father?" He managed to get himself raised up on one elbow. "What happened in Queensland?"

"Oh nothing much. Daddy dearest was just banging his shop assistant. Who, by the way, is my age," She shrugged, "of course he was sorry and promised it wouldn't happen again and mum took him back but he will, he'll do it again."

She sat on the edge of the bed, the can of lighter fluid still in her hand. "You know they say that girls always marry men just like their father." Then she started crying.

Jason sat stunned. Her body was shaking and the tears just seemed to tumble out of her. He wanted to reach over and comfort her but then he didn't know how she would react. He suddenly felt ashamed, felt like he was responsible for all this, this madness, the violence, even her father's infidelities. He knew right there and then that Nancy was over, that this crazy bitch bawling her eyes out, this psycho who'd just threatened to set him on fire, who'd attacked him with a baseball bat, this girl was the only one he wanted and for a moment he wondered if he too wasn't crazy. He tried again to sit up, wanting to hold her and tell her but when he moved he saw stars again. "Cindy…"

She sniffed. "What?"

"I think I might need a doctor."

Fourteen

They were in Dubbo sitting in their motel room, it was Anzac Day and Jason was watching the morning news. Cindy lay in bed, her eyes closed half remembering a dream of Hank running around a football oval. He looked so happy.

"Fucking corporate fucking cunts!"

She sat up quickly. Jason was yelling at the TV screen.

"What's wrong?"

"Those fucking pricks! Isn't anything sacred?" He stood up and turned to her. "These fuckers are on the fucking Kokoda trail big noting themselves as if they've done something heroic and they're wearing their fucking logos on their t-shirts!"

Cindy peered around him nervously. There was a ceremony of some sort on the television. Wreaths being laid, speeches being given, a balding man in a t-shirt talking; on the shirt was a big red 7. He seemed to be the man that Jason was swearing at.

"What's he done wrong?" she asked timidly.

"That prat is just some fucking breakfast announcer wanker who's trekked up there in relative comfort and now gets to talk about the fucking soldiers who died there and he's got his fucking logo everywhere!" Jason was going red in the face. "Who the fuck is he anyway? My fucking grandfather fought in New Guinea, he watched his best mate die up there. Now he's stuck in a home on a fucking pension while these pricks glorify themselves and their fucking networks."

He sat back down and picked up the remote. "Fuck them, granddad's missing half his brain cells, can't wipe his own arse, gets fuck all money from the government and this dickhead's on TV making himself out to be the hero." He turned the set off. "I'm sick of these self-righteous prats who think just cos they got their faces on telly that they represent us. That little prick doesn't represent me or my fucking family. And certainly not my grandfather."

Cindy smiled. "Write a letter then."

"What?"

"You're always complaining. Well, write a letter. Tell the station what you think of them."

Jason stood up. "You know I bloody well will." He walked over to the kitchen bar and picked up the information folder the motel had left for them. "Jesus, wouldn't you know it? You don't get stationery anymore."

"I've never seen stationery in a motel room." Cindy said as she climbed out of the bed.

Jason turned to her. "Well, us old farts can remember the days when you did. Or at least you did in the good motels."

"When were you ever in a good motel?"

Jason stopped for a second. A frown creased his brow. "With Joanne I think," he said softly as the memory flickered. "We were in Melbourne. I remember writing a letter on the letterhead just to impress mum."

Cindy sat back down on the bed. "You never talk about Joanne you know. All you've ever told me is that you were married. Otherwise it's all just little 'first wife' jokes."

She patted the bed, "Tell me about her."

Jason sat down next to her. "I don't know what to say." He blushed a little. "It was a long time ago now, like it was another person."

"How did you meet her?" she asked gently, trying to coax him along.

"At work I guess. I'd been chasing Cheryl for my whole childhood really and never really noticed anyone else. And when we got together it didn't quite go as planned."

"Nothing ever does."

"No, it doesn't does it? Anyway, Joanne just seemed to be there afterwards. We sort of worked around each other, not really admitting that we might like each other, you know…"

Cindy stroked his cheek. "You were such a wimp you know that?"

He was still blushing. "Was? I still am. Anyway, we sort of got together at the pub I think, after work drinks and all that." He shrugged. "We started going out and the next thing I knew, we were engaged."

"You just 'got engaged'?"

"Yeah, I guess so. I don't think we talked about it too much, it just seemed like that was the thing you did. You know, you find the girl, get married, have kids, buy a house, live happily ever after." He turned and looked at her. "We were still kids ourselves, we didn't know any better I guess."

She was watching his eyes, looking for a sign of something, regret maybe, she wasn't sure. "So what went wrong?"

"Like I said, we were still kids. We weren't ready really. I think she just wanted to get out of home and I… well, I think maybe I wanted to prove that I could be a good husband, that I wasn't like my old man."

He stood up suddenly. "I was wrong though, I was just like my old man."

"It wasn't all you was it?"

"Yeah, it was. I mean, her family was a bit odd but that's no excuse."

She was curious now. "What do you mean odd?"

Jason paused, considering the words carefully. "Well, it was a fairly large family, six kids and they were all jealous of each other. They all from youngest to eldest considered that the other kids were spoiled and that they missed out." He was looking at the empty TV screen now. "And Joanne was like that too. I tried to ignore it but it got to me. They had both parents, they had this family unit and yet they didn't seem to appreciate it, they didn't know what they had." He turned back to Cindy. "Don't get me wrong. Dave is a top bloke but I mean Joanne had her mum and dad there for her whole life, you know… and they all did pretty well considering there were six kids… and yet…"

He licked his lips. "Anyway, that wasn't the problem, I was."

She reached up, took his hand in hers. "You were just a kid Jason, you said so yourself." She pulled him closer. "What happened?"

"Well, we had a couple of major fights, she wanted the house a certain way, her life a certain way, she was trying to get away from her family I think… We couldn't live together really but we didn't discover that until we got married."

"You didn't live together first?"

"Oh no. That wasn't the done thing, there was no way her family would have allowed that." He stepped back again, pulling away from her grasp.

"Anyway that's still no excuse for what I did."

Cindy stood up and hugged him. "Which was?"

Jason turned his head away. "I cheated on her," he said quietly. "I picked up a girl at the pub one night after footy." He stepped back and looked at Cindy. "She was the final straw."

Cindy frowned. "It tends to be," she said with an ironic tone.

"Yeah well, she kicked me out and a couple of months later half the wedding gifts showed up on mum's doorstep."

Cindy looked at him, he was smiling. "What's so funny about that?"

"When I say half the wedding gifts I do mean half. Half a crockery set, half a cutlery set, two table settings, two crystal glasses… half of everything except the bread crock which showed up complete but with half a loaf inside." He kissed her on the forehead. "I guess I've always been attracted to crazy women." He pushed her gently back onto the bed. "Now, how about some breakfast in bed?"

"Okay, but no pancakes. And I'll have a half serve of everything."

They'd finished breakfast, Weet-Bix and toast again and were sitting on the double bed playing Travel Scrabble. Jason was losing. He made the word B-O-X.

"Twelve points, now I'm catching up," he muttered sarcastically.

"Did you know Malcolm's been doing kick-boxing?" asked Cindy as she looked at her letters.

"Yeah? Hard to imagine."

"He's bulked up since you last saw him. Lots of gym work and protein shakes."

Jason laughed. "Shit, he'll always be your dweeby little brother to me, protein shakes or not."

Cindy put down her letters – R-A-C-I-N-G – onto the B. "That's a double-word score too, so that's 24 points."

"Okay, I can count." Jason stared at his letters. How come he always got Is and Es? "So, will I see Malc on telly then? Is he any good?"

"I doubt it. Sophie says he's fighting in backyards. It's all illegal."

Jason made I-C-E. He glared at her. "Don't say a word." He picked up another E. "Shit. So backyard, huh? Does he win?"

"He got his nose broken last month. But he said the other guy looked worse." Cindy put down more letters. "M-A-J-O-R-I-T-Y, J and T on triple-letter scores, that's 38 plus 50 bonus points for using all my letters, thank-you."

"Jesus, show some mercy." Jason looked at his block of vowels. "So why does Malcolm do it then? Sounds like he could really get hurt."

"He's trying to impress Dad, I guess, to prove himself. Malcolm was never too smart, you know, and Dad was always disappointed in him." She picked up her letters, smiling, just to goad Jason. "Dad was disappointed in me, too, of course, but I was a girl. Malcolm's his son and heir and as thick as a plank. If *our little accident* Sophie hadn't come along and been gorgeous and smart Christ knows what the olds would have done."

R-E-A-D. Jason mumbled, "Five points," then picked up a Q. The only vowel he didn't have was a U. "So Malc figures getting his head kicked in will impress the old boy."

He shook his head. "Tough way to prove your worth."

"And you wouldn't have done it?" she asked.

"Hell, my old man fucked off before I could read properly. He should be getting his arse kicked to impress me."

Cindy carefully placed her letters. Z-I-N-G-A-R-O. "That's a double letter on the G plus triple-word score, 57 points, I believe."

"Ah, come on, what does that mean?"

"Look it up when you do learn to read."

"Sorry, I only read English." He looked at the score pad, it was time to admit defeat. "Where did you find a word like that anyway?"

"I just read a lot. Not much else I can do these days."

"Well, keep that up and you'll be outside getting some kick-boxing lessons from me."

She laid her hand on his, smiled. "I may be sick, I may be a junkie but I can still kick your arse, boy."

Jason visibly shivered. "You're no junkie," he said quietly, "don't ever say that again."

She kept her hand on his but had to turn her face away. "I'm sorry, Jason… for all this…Hank, the cancer, the drugs…"

"It's not your fault, don't ever think it's your fault."

She turned back to face him, looking him in the eyes. "When they first found the lump I thought…" she paused, "…I thought I deserve this, this is my punishment."

Jason held his breath. He knew exactly how she felt, he knew what she meant. He'd always assumed though that it would happen to him.

Cindy continued, "I thought this was God's way of telling me I should have looked after him better, that I should have been watching him closer."

Jason shook his head. "I'm the one who should be punished. You were inside, I was with him." He choked back a sob. "I was the one who let him run out…"

He faltered, remembering the image of Hank, bright blue T-shirt, jeans one size too big, folded at the cuffs; the ball, bright yellow and green, bouncing past him and him running, giggling…and the car, the Toyota, white, clean, new. He closed his eyes, felt the mucus in his nose and throat, making him want to gag.

"If there is a God, he's a prick. We've done nothing to deserve this." He stood up, cleared his throat and spat into the wastepaper basket. "You've done nothing to deserve this, nothing. Why should you die? What the hell could you have ever done to deserve all this pain?"

His fists were clenching and unclenching. He wanted to strike out, take a swing at something, someone. Find God in a corner bar and brawl with the son of a bitch; give the Almighty a good kicking and see how he liked the pain.

"You've done nothing wrong, Cindy, nothing."

She stayed silent watching him. She could see the tension, his veins throbbing in his temple, his jaw tight, his fists clenching, then loosening, grabbing handfuls of air and trying to squeeze the life out of them.

She stood up slowly, feeling the weariness wash over her, through her, her bones like lead trying to drag her back down. She stepped up to him, took his hand in hers.

"We're not being punished, Jason, I realised that a while ago. We're not being punished, we're being tested."

"What doesn't kill you makes you stronger?" he said tightly.

"Something like that." Still holding his hand she pulled him slowly back to the bed. "I can't be bitter about it anymore, I don't have time. I'm just sorry for dragging you into this, too." She smiled slightly. "I thought I'd got rid of you once and for all but you always come back."

"I'm a hard man to shake off." He lay down next to her. "Like a mangy pit bull… you keep shaking and I just keep holding on."

She ran a hand through his hair. "Well, I'm glad you did. I don't think I could do this without you."

She sat up suddenly, grabbing at brochures on the bedside cupboard. "Let's go to the zoo. I haven't been to one for years. I want to see the animals one last time." She stood up, felt giddy and sat back on the bed.

"Maybe tomorrow," Jason said quietly.

"No, there are no more tomorrows. I don't have the luxury of tomorrows, let's do it now." She stood up again, slower this time. "I'll just go to the bathroom, then we'll go."

Jason knew what she was doing in the bathroom but he pretended he didn't. He didn't want to think about her shooting up, about the needle he'd find in the bin later, carefully wrapped up in plastic, a small nib of foam on the point. He wondered where she got the foam but decided not to ask. He preferred ignorance right now. He just wanted to pretend it was all still okay, that Cindy would get better and they'd come back home after their brief holiday in Queensland to a new start, a new life together. He wasn't sure how much longer he could fool himself.

Cindy sat on the toilet, flicked the tissue into the bin and relaxed. The needle sat on the sink, its usefulness over, for now at least. She felt good, warm and secure in a cocoon of painless bliss.

She could forget about the aches for the moment, the small jolts of pain in every joint, the shocks like electricity, which would hit her now and again, passing through her frame, pausing only to sap the little energy she had left. No, none of that while the dope ran up her arm and into her bloodstream, just warmth and luxury and velvet kisses in her veins.

Mechanically she pulled another tissue out of the box and dabbed at the spot of blood on her arm. Something fell into place then, a memory popped up unexpectedly. The mechanical way she dabbed at the blood; her mum wiping away a trickle of blood from her lip, her dad standing there, breathing heavily, saying "sorry" over and over.

She trembled. Where did that come from? She could taste copper in her mouth again.

Jason had to admit he was impressed. He didn't like zoos, couldn't see the point once you were past about 12 or 13 of watching large animals take a dump in a small cage.

But this was different. This was 300 hectares of open space, fields, ranges – there was some scope here for your imagination. He just wished he still had some.

Cindy seemed to be enjoying herself though and for that he was glad. Through her eyes he could almost become that 12-year-old again, the boy who was fascinated with wild animals and their bodily functions, with the simple thrill of life, of minor discoveries and their inherent trails to bigger things.

Once again he found himself wondering what he was going to do without her. She had always been the zany one, the wild thing prone to acts of childish self-indulgence, poking and farting, kiddy jokes and who cares about the consequences?

While Jason had his own moments of self-indulgence and not caring for the consequences they were more selfish and self-destructive and usually involved women and alcohol.

Cindy was having fun, wanted a good time; Jason just wanted.

He pulled her close not wanting to let go for fear of her never coming back. He had a vision of her melting into the crowd or walking away or, and he thought this more probable, the fear she would simply run into the hills and spend her last days with the animals, scavenging for food scraps among the lion cubs or wallowing in the mud with the hippos.

She turned to him, gave him a peck on the cheek and smiled. "Aren't they wonderful?"

He tightened his grip. "Did you come here when you were 15?" he asked, still not letting her go.

"Only for a little while. Dad wanted to get to the observatory so we didn't get much time here at all."

"Observatory?"

"Up at Coonabarabran. Something Springs it was called. Dad's into the stars and shit."

I saw stars, she thought, the night he hit me for smoking dope at school. Cindy shook her head. Did that really happen?

"You okay?" Jason asked.

"Huh? Oh, yeah…just having a flashback or something." She pointed to the right. "Look, elephants!" Jason smiled. Her voice had almost squeaked with excitement.

After the zoo, Jason had suggested the old jail. He wanted to see the gallows but Cindy was exhausted.

"You're morbid, Myers, you know that? Morbid."

"No, I'm not. Anyway I thought you'd like it. Think about all those well-hung men."

He got a punch in the arm. "I like my men with smaller nooses." She slid her hand into his pocket. "Any loose change in there?"

He grinned. "Keep fishing you might come across a dollar or two."

"That's all I need."

Jason didn't get to the jail.

In the morning Cindy felt too tired, too drained for the side trip to the observatory so they decided to head straight to Tamworth. If the HR hadn't blown a welch plug at Gunnedah, Jason would never have been reunited with his father.

Fifteen

Jason noticed the leak when they'd pulled over for coffee at Coonabarabran. It didn't look too serious though and he figured if he took it slow he'd get to Tamworth before it could cause any real trouble, then he'd have it looked at. He was wrong. The plug blew just outside Gunnedah. An hour later a tow truck deposited them at Smithy's workshop.

"Nice lookin' car, mate," said Smithy admiringly, "you obviously been lookin' after it."

"Not me, my stepfather. He likes the old Holdens."

Smithy wiped his hands on his overalls then popped the car's bonnet. "Yep, welch plugs blown, just like I thought. Lucky you didn't boil the engine, lad, very lucky." He stood back up, looked at Jason. "There's a day's work there, mate, at least."

Jason smiled. "I may not own the car but I do know a little about it. That isn't a day's work. Couple of hours sure but no more than that."

Smithy frowned, then sighed. "Okay but it still won't be ready till late tomorrow. I've got a Falcon on the hoist gettin' its brakes done, a coupla services booked in and I'm down one mechanic."

"Tell you what," said Jason, "get it done by, say, 10.30 tomorrow morning and we'll pay cash. No paperwork, no taxman."

Smithy laughed. "I reckon you got a deal, son. What's your name?"

"Jason, Jason Myers."

"Myers, huh? You know, you look just like him. I thought you did when you first walked in, but I didn't want to say anything in case I was wrong."

"Look like who?"

"Why, your old man, of course. Frank Myers."

Jason's mouth dropped open.

Cindy said, "His father's here?"

"Well, if his father's Frank Myers, and by the look on the boy's face he is, then yep, his father's here."

"Where?" asked Jason. "This time of day, he's probably just finishing his rounds…"

"Rounds?"

"Yep. He's a sales rep, car parts and the like." Smithy pointed to a small pile of boxes and blister packs on a workbench, light globes, fuses, electrical wiring tumbling out and covering it. "Give him half hour and I reckon you'll catch him at the Regal. Loves his beer does Frank."

Cindy looked at Jason. "Do you want to see him? I mean, if it is him."

Jason shrugged not sure what to say. "I guess so. I really don't know."

Smithy interrupted. "Well, either way, young Myers, I'll have your car done by 10.30 tomorrow morning. But I'm guessin' you haven't seen Frank for a while…would seem a shame to waste this opportunity."

Smithy turned and headed back towards the waiting Falcon, leaving the couple standing in the doorway still undecided.

Cindy called after him, "We'll see you in the morning then." He raised an arm in acknowledgment. She looked to Jason. "Well?"

"I guess we may as well go to the Regal. We'll need to find a room somewhere anyway."

There were five people in the bar when they walked in; Frank Myers wasn't one of them. "C'mon let's go."

"No, we'll stay." Cindy sat down at a corner table. "I'll have a scotch and Coke, thanks." Jason stood there, looking down at her. "Well?"

"I don't know about this, Cindy."

"Make it a half-scotch then."

"You know what I mean."

She pointed to the bar. "Okay, I'm going."

He came back with a scotch and a pint of beer for himself. "What am I going to say to him?"

"I don't know. 'Where have you been you bastard?'"

"You're not helping."

Cindy shrugged. "Look, you don't want to waste this chance, Jason. You might not get another."

He sat down next to her. "I just don't know Cindy, I don't know. When he left I thought it was me, I thought I'd done something."

"Isn't that standard though? All kids think that."

"I know, I know. But Bradley and I just didn't know what else to think." Jason shrugged, "We loved him you know, like only boys can. And then he upped and left. We had no idea why."

She touched his arm gently. "Well, maybe today you can ask him."

"Oh yeah, I'm sure that would go down well. Hey dad, how are you? By the way, what the fuck went wrong?"

Cindy smiled. "Well, it would be a start."

Jason put his glass to his lips, felt the cooling ale slide down his throat, taking his time and wondering just what he would say, what he could say. He didn't even know if he really wanted to meet his father. It had been so long, this man who had created him, had sired him and then left him; could he even call him dad? Dave had been his father really not Frank. He had certainly been there longer, he'd got both Bradley and Jason through the hard stuff, the fights, the fears, through puberty and the girls and the chaos. Frank wasn't there when Bradley broke his arm at footy, Dave was. Frank wasn't there when Naomi Wells claimed Jason was the father of her baby, Dave was the man who talked her brothers into not beating Jason up, Dave was the man who got her to admit that Johnno was in fact the culprit. Where was Frank then? Where was Frank when mum had the cancer scare, when they first found that lump in her breast, where was he, his father? He wasn't there, Dave was.

"Shit," he said out loud, "why couldn't Bradley have found him?"

"Because he wasn't looking," Cindy said softly, her hand still resting on his.

They sat in silence, sipping their drinks and watching the afternoon regulars start to drift in. A heavyset man in a white shirt, dark pants and tie came through the door.

Jason caught his breath. Frank Myers had aged, put on weight – a lot of weight – but Jason could still see him in there, the face of the man who'd put him to bed and read him stories about Tarzan and Robin Hood; the face that haunted the one or two black-and-white photos his mum still had lying in the bottom of the linen cupboard; the face of the man who had deserted them when Jason was 7½ years old.

Frank's beer was poured and waiting before he even got to the bar. Jason watched every step he took to get to it.

"Is that him?" whispered Cindy.

"Yeah, it's him."

"Are you going to talk to him?"

Jason looked at Frank as he settled onto a stool, picked up the pot and drained it in one long swallow. The bartender was already pouring another.

"I don't know. I don't know what to say." He turned back to Cindy. "How do I do it? Hi, remember me? I'm your son."

"It's a start." Cindy pushed her empty glass across to him. "Get us another drink and you can at least get a closer look."

Reluctantly, Jason went back to the bar. He stood down the bar and watched his father talking to another guy in similar attire, another sales rep, he guessed. They were joking about some secretary's short skirt. It was definitely his father. He took the drinks and went back to the table.

"Well? Are you going to talk to him?"

"Yeah, yeah, don't rush me... I'm trying to work out what to say."

Jason sat nursing his drink trying to work up the courage to confront his father, trying to come up with an opening sentence that didn't sound like gibberish, some way to introduce himself to the man who had abandoned him so long ago. In the end it didn't matter, Smithy solved the problem for him.

Smithy came through from the other bar, walked up to Frank and said, "Hey, Frank, met your boy today. Hell, there he is over there." Smithy waved. "Jason, come on over here." Father and son looked at each other.

Cindy jabbed Jason in the ribs. "Come on, let's go and say hello to Dad."

Frank was stunned. This man standing in front of him was supposed to be his son. The seven-year-old tearaway he'd watched riding his bike precariously around the block for the first time, the kid who he'd tried in vain to teach to mark a ball without dropping it, the kid who drew him pictures of bears to take to work.

He tried to put the child into this adult. Take away the long hair, the solid frame, imagine a few more freckles across the nose – it was the eyes and the shape of the mouth though that told him all he needed, this was his boy.

He held out his hand. "Hello, son, it's been a long time."

Reluctantly, Jason took his hand. "Hello, Frank."

Smithy stood there, grinning. "As soon as I laid eyes on him, Frank, I thought, hell that looks like Frank Myers. You never told us you had a son, Frank."

Frank put his hand on Smithy's shoulder. "Patrick, I haven't seen my son for many years. Do you think perhaps we could have some time together… alone?"

"Huh…oh yeah. Sure, Frank…I'll just be in the other bar."

"Thank you, Patrick." Frank turned his attention back to Jason. "So, son who is this lovely lady on your arm? You've certainly picked a beautiful woman to be your partner."

Jason flinched. "Cindy meet Frank, my long-lost father."

"Delighted," Cindy smiled. "It's a pleasure to finally meet you, Frank. I've heard a lot about you."

Frank laughed. "And I'm sure very little of it was complimentary."

Jason looked down at his feet, shuffled, then said, "Should we sit down, maybe?"

Frank gestured towards the dining area. "I have a table booked for dinner later. We may as well take a seat now." They sat and Frank ordered a round of drinks. "So, tell me, Jason, what brings you up this way? Employment, a vacation?"

Jason picked up his beer, took a long drink. "I'm taking Cindy home to Brisbane."

"It's a driving holiday," interrupted Cindy, "we're taking the scenic route."

"Ah yes, Jason always did like going for long drives. It was a Sunday ritual actually, a long drive through the countryside."

"As if you remember," said Jason, already regretting this meeting. He just didn't feel comfortable sitting with this man, this smooth-talking salesman who thought nothing it seemed of his absence from Jason's life for the past 28 years.

"Now, now, son, I know you're angry with me. And I know you feel you have every reason to be so but we're all adults here, we don't need to be bitter." He reached across the table and put his hand on top of Jason's.

Jason pulled away. "I'm not bitter, Frank I got over that a long time ago."

Cindy sat quietly watching the two of them as they sparred with words and gestures, both trying to appear casual about this chance reunion, both trying to pretend it didn't really matter what the other man thought.

Despite what Jason was saying, despite Dave's efforts to be his father, she knew Jason had missed Frank these 28 years, she knew he still craved his father's affection, his approval, his love. Now that he had the chance though to bridge the gap, to make some moves towards getting to know his father again, he seemed unprepared, unwilling to admit his need for that affection, that approval.

"I'm not your son Frank, you gave that and me up a long time ago."

"Don't be like that, Jason. It just had to be. Your mother and I simply weren't compatible."

Jason's voice rose. "No. But you and that student teacher were. Or was it the real estate agent?"

Frank sat stunned. He wasn't sure what he'd expected out of this chance reunion, this random meeting with his offspring but it wasn't this. He knew the boy wouldn't exactly greet him with warmth, hugs and an open invitation to his house and home, but he was surprised at the bitterness, the rancour he sensed at the table now.

"They were symptoms son, nothing more. Your mother and I were already having difficulties. You can't blame my relationship with Sarah for my leaving."

"So who do I blame? Me? Mum? What happened then…to cause these… difficulties?"

"Nothing is that simple I'm afraid, son. It's not a matter of just saying this was the reason…or that…"

Frank picked up his glass, emptying it with one gulp, then poured another from the jug on the table. "We live in a society that believes that God is dead and that Elvis is alive…"

"And what the hell does that mean?" Jason stood up, not caring about the other bar patrons who were now watching them.

"I'm simply trying to say that nothing is clear-cut, nothing is simple. Life is complicated, son, very complicated."

Frank didn't even see the punch. He fell back off his chair, rose and was punched again. Jason stood over him. "The first one was for Mum, the second was for me and Bradley. If you stand up I'll give you another for the grandson you never even met."

Frank slowly stood up, pushing the chair aside. "Go ahead, son, if it makes you feel better, you can hit me again."

Jason raised his fist, looked at this man standing before him, blood trickling from his lip, then dropped his hands to his side. "No, it doesn't make me feel any better. I wish it did." He turned and walked out of the dining room. "Come on, Cindy, I think it's time to go."

Frank stood there and watched them leave. He thought briefly about following them, of calling out to his son but he didn't. Instead he sat down, signaled for a fresh jug and studied the menu. The steak looked good but he found he no longer had an appetite.

Sixteen

The motel room was that dull tan they always were, not quite woodgrain, not quite wooden bench but a recognisable shade of bland. The bedspread was cream, dulled by years of washing though, the carpet dark but unremarkable, no pattern, just there for you to walk on as you came in weary from your travels, your travails.

On the wall was a large photo of a wolf reflected perfectly in the lake it was drinking from. It was a clean room though, towels fresh, new kettle, water in the fridge, paper strip across the toilet seat to assure you of its cleanliness.

There was no mini bar though so while Cindy shot up in the bathroom, Jason went and bought a six-pack. When he came back she was sitting on the bed staring at the wolf.

"You okay?" he asked as he put the six-pack less one in the fridge. Cindy didn't move, just sat staring at the animal on the wall.

Jason wondered if in fact the photo was real, if the wolf had really been drinking at this watering hole, sating its thirst while its twin was reflected perfectly staring straight back – not yin and yang, just yin duplicated.

He couldn't fathom the photographer's luck to have been there at that precise moment. Had he been waiting patiently for days on end, camped out at this lake knowing that eventually the wolf would come or was it just pure luck, blind chance – like walking into a bar and finding your long-lost father after too many years.

Or was the whole photo fake? Computer graphics and cut and paste, offering us a wildlife scene that could never exist, a fake wild animal to go with the fake woodgrain, the fake servility of the staff, the fake hopes in the Gideons in the top drawer.

He asked again, "You okay?"

She nodded. "Mm just tired."

He sat next to her and watched the wolf as he drank. Neither talked, both lost in their own drug of choice until the six-pack was gone and the rush was over. Then they climbed wearily into bed, both sleeping fitfully until morning.

Jason didn't want to go to Smithy's to pick up the car. He was sure that after his display last night at the pub the car would still be sitting in the street, dripping water, insects suicided on the grill, chip packets on the floor, welch plug still sealed in its box waiting for someone else to put it in. He was wrong. The car was on the street but it was clean, inside and out, plug replaced, belts adjusted, air pressure checked, new oil filter, one rear light globe replaced and a new spare tire in the boot.

Smithy was inside drinking coffee. "Ah, young Jason, your car's all done, finished her just a few minutes ago." He handed Jason the paperwork.

"What's going on? All I wanted was the welch plug fixed, I can't afford all the other stuff."

Smithy laughed. "That's a receipt, lad, not a bill. Frank's already paid for it all."

"He did what? After what I said last night, after what I did."

"Oh yeah, he had a beautiful shiner this morning, was quite proud of it, I think. I know you don't think much of Frank, and I don't know enough of your story to know if you're right or wrong…" He sipped his coffee, grimacing at its sweetness. "Too much sugar…your old man, in his own way, is a top bloke. Fatherhood may not be his strong suit but mateship is."

Jason had to lean back on a bench. He felt giddy, flushed. "I don't know what to say." He looked again at the receipt, turned and looked out at the car. "I hit him and he pays for my car to get fixed."

"That's about it," smiled Smithy.

"Shit, I should have shot the bastard, I might have got a new car then."

Coffee sprayed the floor as Smithy burst out laughing. "Fuck, you're Frank's boy alright."

As they left Gunnedah, Cindy turned to Jason, "What was it like? Hitting him,

I mean?" She paused, bit her lip. "I mean…did you feel better afterwards?" Jason watched the road, saying nothing, just trying to relive the punch, the feeling as his father toppled back off his chair, then that second punch, the one he threw without even realising it himself. He smiled then. "I don't know, confusing I guess. I knew I was going to hit him as soon as I saw him walk into the bar. I just knew it."

He looked at her, there was no expression on her face so he didn't know how she was taking all of this. "When I finally did hit him I felt relief, I think…relief that it was out of the way, that he was out of the way…"

He stopped abruptly, looking at a shape appearing on the horizon. There was a car and a figure standing next to it. The figure looked familiar.

"You're shitting me," he said quietly, "you're fucking shitting me."

His father was standing next to a late-model Ford, thumb out, trying to hitch a lift.

For a moment he thought of just driving by, ignoring the spare parts sales rep stranded on the highway, the spare parts father who had left him stranded so many birthdays ago, so many Christmases past with nary a card or a present, just faded black-and-white photos and a surname he'd stubbornly clung to as if his future depended on his birthright, but he didn't. Reluctantly, he eased his foot off the accelerator and pulled up in front of his father's Ford.

Frank saw the car coming up the highway and stepped forward, thumb out. The Ford had simply run out of fuel and he'd cursed himself for his own stupidity for a full 10 minutes before climbing out to wait on the road for a lift. All he hoped for was that the driver would get him to a service station up ahead or even maybe back to Smithy's.

As the car came closer though he thought about stepping back.

"Get in, Frank," said Jason, "I won't hit you."

Frank stood, one hand paused to open the door. "Are you sure, son? I mean about the ride, not the fighting."

"Just get in," said Cindy, "he's a pussycat really."

Frank pointed to his eye. "Oh yes a real pussycat this lad."

He opened the door. "I just need to get to a petrol station, son, then I'll be out of your hair once again."

Jason turned to watch his father clamber into the back seat. "I'm sorry Frank, I shouldn't have hit you last night."

"It's alright son, I understand."

"You do?" asked Cindy.

Frank looked at her. She looked so tired, frail. He didn't have to ask to know this was her last trip home. He decided not to lie.

"No, I don't really. But I guess I wasn't that surprised either. There's a lot of his mother in him, a real fighter."

"A real nagger too."

He laughed.

Jason started the car. "You two finished? Where to Frank?"

"Smithy's? I just need petrol."

"Isn't there anywhere ahead?"

"Sorry but it's probably more expedient to go back."

Cindy turned to face Frank.

"How could you forget petrol, Frank? You seem so organised."

"I guess I was distracted, young lady. My mind was on other things," he shrugged, "these things happen."

Cindy smiled. "Oh yeah like you get punched every day by your son."

"No, you are correct, it's not an everyday occurrence."

"Well, it should be," said Jason only half-joking.

"So how did you end up down this way, Frank? Jason told me you were in Darwin."

"That was a very long time ago. I move around as the work requires. This position is based in Dubbo actually. I travel between there and Lismore, servicing the motor market, spare parts and the like."

"Do you like it?"

"I enjoy it, yes. Plenty of characters like Smithy. It makes the position… interesting I suppose is the word. Yes, interesting."

"And family?" Jason asked carefully, quietly, one eye on the road, one eye on the bulky form in his rear-vision mirror.

"Yes, I wondered when that question would rear its head." Frank shifted in his seat, straining against the seat belt as it cut into his ample chest. "There was. I remarried but alas my traveling did not make for a settled life," he raised his hand. "and before you ask, son, there was no one else, just the job."

Jason thought there was a hint of sadness in those last few words. "Kids?" He tried to sound casual.

"A girl, your half-sister Cassie. She's a beautiful girl, 14 now."

"Where…where is she?" His voice croaked out the words through a suddenly dry throat.

"In Darwin still with her mother. I talk to them, send birthday cards, letters…"

Jason felt a pain, a shift of something in his chest, it hurt and he had to blink tears from his eyes. "Does she know about me? About your sons, your previous life?"

"A little. I told her of you and Bradley's existence. She is aware of having half-brothers, of another family."

"That's something, I guess."

"And you son? You said something about a grandson after the blow that resulted in this eye I believe?"

Jason turned to Cindy. "You can tell him," he said almost inaudibly.

Cindy swallowed. "We had a boy, his name was Hank but…" she took a deep breath, "there was an accident. He died when he was four."

Jason could see his father's face in the mirror. Frank grimaced.

"I'm so sorry, so sorry for both of you." He hesitated. "I wish... I wish I had known him, known you both." He went silent and stared at the back of his son's head, not knowing what to say now.

Jason felt his temper flare but stopped himself. "Life is complicated Frank, you said that yourself. We had him for a little while at least and we'll never forget him."

"Sometimes son, that is about the best you can do." He reached over and put his hand on his son's shoulder. "I know you won't believe me but I never forgot about you or Bradley, I never stopped thinking about you both. I guess I was scared though that you had forgotten about me."

"I tried to believe me, I tried to." Jason reached a hand back and touched his father's. "But I guess I couldn't."

He grinned and took a quick look back at his father. "You know, every time I smell Old Spice I still think of you. Of course you're much thinner in my head though."

Cindy giggled. "So that's why you wear it. I always wondered."

Jason blushed. "No, I just happen to like it, that's all."

"And your mother?" Franks' voice dropped a little.

"She remarried. Dave, a nice bloke," Jason answered quietly, "he stuck around despite Bradley and me doing our best to fuck it all up."

"She's happy then?"

"As happy as mum can be." Jason took another quick glance back at his father. "Dave's working in the city but she refuses to move so I guess she's a single mum again technically."

"Or at least a single grandma," chipped in Cindy.

Frank looked puzzled. "You?"

"No," she laughed, "Bradley and Rachel are about to have a kid."

"Sorry, should have told you. Slipped my mind," apologised Jason as Smithy's came into view. "Well, there it is. Will you be okay?"

Frank nodded. "Yes, Patrick will fix me up and take me back to the car."

They pulled up outside the garage. Frank clambered out of the HR, stuck his head through the open passenger window. "Thank you Jason. I appreciate you going out of your way for me."

Jason got out of the car. "Frank, I'm sorry for hitting you."

"No," interrupted Frank, "I'm sorry. You've grown up to be a fine young man and I'm sorry I missed that." They shook hands. "Take care of yourself, son."

"You, too, Frank."

Frank pulled a business card from his shirt pocket. "Here. Call me if you ever want any more Old Spice. I can get it wholesale."

Frank walked inside, Jason got back into the car; neither looked back.

Seventeen

Cindy and Jason drove in silence. They passed Frank's car sitting on the side of the road and Cindy turned to look at it as it diminished in the distance.

When it was just a tiny haze she said, "Did he ever hit you?"

Jason jumped slightly. "Sorry, what did you say?"

"Did he ever hit you?"

"I don't think so. He may have smacked us occasionally but I can't remember anything." He glanced over. "Why?"

"I'm starting to remember things," said Cindy nervously, "things I'd sort of…I don't know…forgotten about I guess or maybe never even considered, things I haven't thought about for a long time"

She unclipped her seat belt, moved closer to Jason. "When I was little my father used to smack me, which I guess was standard stuff for the time but it progressed. I've never really thought about it until now, I just considered it normal."

Jason put one hand on hers. "And it wasn't?"

"I don't know. It was to us."

"What did he do? Just smack you, use a belt?"

"He would hit us, me, Mum, Malcolm…he'd punch us…with his fists." She shifted closer still, her body up against him now. "I never really thought about it, I just assumed everyone was disciplined like that."

"Like what?" Jason asked cautiously.

Cindy could feel her cheeks burning. "I don't know. Closed fists, slaps, kicks…he gave me a black eye once, gave Mum a couple of fat lips, bruises…that sort of thing."

Jason didn't know what to say. Cindy's father didn't seem capable of this…this violence. He'd always been fairly quiet around Jason, thoughtful, old-fashioned. No dirty jokes or bravado, a fairly normal middle-class father with the possible exception of his lousy taste in football teams and ties.

"And this went on for how long?"

Cindy was cuddled into his side now and he slipped an arm around her. "I guess always. We weren't naughty kids really, we were just kids. It was later on I got out of hand, but then we were just normal kids."

"Why didn't you say something? Why didn't you at least tell me?"

"I didn't even think about it," she shifted, pushed his arm away. "We just thought it was normal, that everyone got punished like that. We didn't know any different I guess.

If you see it every day, if you get hit every day you just assume that that's how it works, that's how parents behave, how they're supposed to behave. I had nothing to compare it to. If that's the way it is, if that's the way it always seems to be then you just adjust to it, you accept it as the way things are."

She was sorry now that she had even told him about it. Every question seemed accusatory, every word blaming her. Luckily he sensed her mood.

"I'm sorry," he said, "I'm not trying to blame you. I'm trying to understand what you're telling me, I'm trying to picture your father as an abuser, a wife basher, a child basher." He put his arm back around her. "I believe you, Cindy. I don't think you're lying. I'm just trying to…I don't know…digest all this information, make sense of it." He pecked her on the cheek. "But I don't doubt you at all, okay?"

She stayed close to him as they continued driving but there was a tension in her spine now, a spring coiled tight and he kept quiet, just hoping that holding her close as they passed the spectacular rock formations and freefalling landscape was enough to allay her fears, to make her realise that he did believe her, that he was on her side.

She relaxed a little. "When I went to Queensland, when I took Hank…"

"Yeah…" he said slowly.

"There was some stuff I didn't tell you."

"You mean besides your father's affair?"

She nodded. "There were other things happening. I just didn't realise it."

He felt her tensing up again. "Like what?"

"Well," Cindy paused, considered her words carefully. "Mum had a broken wrist. She told me she'd fallen in the garden."

"You don't think she did?" he asked, trying not to sound accusing or suspicious.

"Not now that I think back, now that I'm recalling things." She sat up again.

"See, she had some bruises too but she said she didn't know where she got them. Probably banging around the yard, she said." Cindy stared out the window trying not to look at Jason. "I should have put two and two together. I mean he always hit us as kids and like I said, mum copped her share too. Why didn't I piece it together?"

Jason put his hand on her leg. "You couldn't have known Cindy. You just said that you didn't really even remember it. Besides she's a grown woman, she's not your responsibility."

"Isn't she? She's my mother and I didn't even think about the fact he was still hitting her. I didn't even consider it." She slapped the window in frustration. "Hell, I'd pretty much forgotten about it all. And Sophie's still at home too."

Jason looked at her. "Does he hit her?"

"I honestly don't know. But why would he change? She didn't say anything but then she wasn't around much either. When dad was home she always seemed to make herself scarce."

He pulled her back close and let her cuddle into him. Her spine was still tight, brittle and for a moment her feared that she would snap under the pressure. He relaxed his grip a little but she pulled his arm back tight around her. "I don't know what to think Jason, I just don't know."

"You can't blame yourself, you were just a kid then. What could you have done?"

She shook her head. "But I do blame myself. Don't you see? I do blame myself."

As they neared Tamworth she started to doze, a light sleep that uncoiled her spine, relaxing her as she molded herself into his side. He decided not to stop, not wanting to wake her. He hoped the petrol would hold out until Uralla.

Cindy woke slowly, groggily and sitting up realised with a start she was alone in the car. She had no idea where though.

It was raining, grey and dull outside and the rain was falling heavily, water bombs hitting the roof, window and bonnet. She looked out the window at the land, the rocks, the horizon. She could see clouds hanging low, pulsating in a dull, vicious manner, threatening to flood this land, the fields, nature ready to wash away all the signs of man, of civilisation.

She curled up in a ball and rocked back and forth gently, wondering where Jason was, where she was, why she was alone. Her thoughts bounced briefly towards a taste but she'd left her gear in the boot and she didn't have the courage to get out of the car to retrieve it. Closing her eyes, she rocked herself back to sleep hoping it would all be okay when she woke up again.

She dreamed of a great flood washing away her street, saw her mother standing on the roof clutching a tea towel and calling her. Her dinner was ready. Cindy was paddling furiously through the flood waters trying to reach her front door when Sophie bobbed up next to her, sitting in a small boat and dressed in a hospital gown, the drip still hanging from her arm. "Thanks for the help sis," she said snarling before the outboard motor kicked in and the boat sped off. "No," Cindy shouted, "it wasn't my fault." Then she saw her dad walking across the water, his belt in his hand. "Young lady you're late again." Cindy stopped paddling, waited for the waters to claim her but something was keeping her afloat, stopping her descent into the swirling waters. She looked down through the grey-blue foam and saw Jason. He was wearing the suit he'd worn at the funeral, the one he'd borrowed from Dave. He was holding the baseball bat. "Here honey, try this…"

She reached for it but couldn't get a grip. Her father was striding ever closer, the belt seeming to get larger and larger. She wondered where Malcolm was. Then she heard his voice and looked up. He was sitting on the roof of their house eating a sandwich. "Hurry up sis, you're gonna miss tea." Sophie was sitting next to him, still in her hospital gown, "Yeah come on slow coach, or we'll eat it all." Then someone or something touched her cheek...

Jason found her asleep still curled up by the passenger door. A line of dribble glistened down one cheek. He wiped it off gently, she twitched. He ran his finger across her cheek again and her eyes slowly opened. The rain had stopped, she was in the car, her father wasn't coming to get her and Jason wasn't in his borrowed funeral suit.

"You're here." She grabbed his arm. "Where were you? I thought you'd left me."

Gently, he pulled her to him. "Didn't you see the note? We ran out of petrol, I had to walk."

She looked at his hair, his jacket; he was wet, soaking. "You got wet."

He had to laugh. "Nothing gets past you, does it?"

"I was so scared, Jason. I woke up and you were gone and the rain..." She shivered. "I thought I was dead."

"Not while I'm here," he said so quietly that she almost missed it, "not while I'm here."

They stopped in Armidale for coffee and a break. At the cafe Cindy pieced together what had happened. "So you thought we could make it to Uralla?"

"Uh huh." He opened a sugar sachet, poured it into his coffee.

"But we didn't."

"That's about it." He stirred the coffee.

She smiled gently. "Like father like son."

He flicked his empty sugar packet at her. "Gimme a break. I was trying not to wake you."

She put her head down. "I think I would have rather been woken up. I was so scared when I was alone in the car, so scared."

"I'm sorry. I didn't think you would react like that, I should have waited." He picked up his coffee then tasting it, winced. "Shit, can't I get a good coffee anywhere? Fucking students."

"What do students have to do with it?"

"Look around. All the bloody employees here are students, part-timers." He put the cup down. "I hate fucking uni students."

Cindy looked at him across the table, frowned. "Why? What have they done to you?"

Jason picked up another sugar sachet. "They're just a bunch of smart-arse time-wasters. None of them work, they just get BAs in bloody art and bullshit and we pay for it. If they are trying to be doctors or something they complain about paying for the privilege! Jesus, how much money will they make out of us once they open their fucking surgeries anyway?"

"Well, they're working here."

"This isn't work. Christ, they can't even make a good cup of coffee." He stirred in the sugar.

"You're full of shit, you know that."

He smiled slowly. "Yeah, I know."

"So why do you really dislike students?" she asked, as she tasted her own coffee, trying hard not to grimace.

"I don't know. They just give me the shits. They're always complaining about their rights, their fucking education but they don't seem to be doing much with it anyway. I mean a PhD in comics or fucking post-modern literature? That'll come in handy in the factory." He noticed her trying not to screw her face up as she drank her coffee but said nothing. "I'm probably just jealous. I got kicked out of school when I was fifteen, I didn't even get the option of going to uni. Hell no one I knew did. But they seem to take it for granted and then they want everyone else to pay for it. I guess it's just that they seem to want it all for nothing. Fuck 'em. I've got to work for the shit I want, why can't they?"

"But don't you believe in free education?"

Jason grunted, "Well, yeah I do… to a point. Like I said, who needs a PHD in bloody postmodern comics?! And why do I pay for it?"

Cindy had to laugh. "You hate paying your taxes anyway. You're always trying to get out of it." She put her cup down. "I didn't get to go to uni either but you don't see me whining about them. Anyway, what would you do at university?"

"Well, I'd learn to make better fucking coffee for a start."

Cindy knew they would be over the border soon, back in Queensland, back into her parents' care. It would only really take a good solid day or so of driving to reach home if Jason really put his mind to it and his foot down. She was no longer sure though that she wanted to go home. Knowing how short her life was, feeling it all drain out slowly like a tap with a leaky washer, drip-drip-drip, her life down the drain; knowing this, feeling this, she wanted to be here on the road with Jason; just traveling, little to no responsibility left, stopping where and whenever they wanted; time no longer important except perhaps the need to enjoy what she had left.

Stoned, high, wasted and letting the road take them where it may, except it was taking her home to a house she was no longer sure she wanted to visit. She talked Jason into staying the night in Armidale. They ordered in a pizza, she got wasted, he got smashed and they cuddled up and watched boxing on Austar, cheering the heavyweights as they battered each other, throwing wild punches, blind haymakers, hoping something might land.

After the fights were over and the TV turned off, Cindy lay back on the pillow, "Jason?"

"Yeah?" he muttered as he dropped an empty beer can into the small bin next to the fridge and considered whether he really needed another.

"I think we should talk… about Nancy and everything," she said slowly.

Jason decided he would need that beer. "What is there to say now?" He opened the can and sat on the end of the bed. He was sure that the quilt cover was exactly the same as the one in Gunnedah. "I forgave you, you forgave me… we're even."

"It doesn't work that way Jason, we both know that."

He shrugged. "What do you want to know then?"

"It isn't what I want to know, it's… well… it's what you don't know." She sat up and beckoned him. "There's more to it all Jason, more to everything I guess."

He crawled up the bed and sat next to her. He really didn't want to talk but he could sense that she needed it. "Okay then, talk to me."

Cindy swallowed and took a deep breath. "I told you about dad and mum, about the affair, the fights, mum's wrist…"

"Yeah?" he said wondering what the hell could be left.

"I didn't tell you though why I came home." She put her head down not wanting to face him.

"You mean that wasn't enough?"

"I hit Hank," she said haltingly, "I slapped him."

Jason took her hand. "Cindy, I smacked Hank too, it's not a good thing but we didn't know any better."

"No," she shook her head, "I hurt him, I didn't just smack him as a punishment, it was harder than that, like I was taking something out on him. I scared him and I scared myself. I didn't even know where it was coming from, I hadn't connected the dots yet, but I was scared." She took a deep breath, "Or maybe I did know but I wasn't admitting it. There was a lot going on you know and I wasn't facing any of it."

He stopped her. "No Cindy you are not like your father. Don't even think it. You said it yourself, it was normal to you, you didn't know any different."

"I understood enough to know I didn't want to raise Hank the same way." She sat up, the words were tumbling out now. "I came home to see you, to tell you that I wanted us to be together, to be a family. I didn't want to be like my dad, I didn't want to hit my kids, I didn't want Hank to be scared, I wanted us to be happy together."

Jason could see now where this was going. "And I wasn't there for you was I?"

"No but it wasn't really your fault. I thought it was at the time. I hated you so much for not waiting for me, for taking off with Nancy, for leaving me and Hank."

"But what was it about Nancy? What made her any different than anyone else? I mean we both had other… relationships, people, whatever we wanted to call them. Was it just the timing, Hank, your father? I never understood exactly what was going on, what she had done to you."

"I guess I just wanted us to be together. I wanted Hank to be happy, to have a family. I was so wired, so stressed. I should have just gone away, taken some time to think it all out but I didn't. I saw you and her and you both looked so happy together and she was so together, so calm. I think I was jealous more than anything."

Jason suddenly felt ashamed, "I should have realised, I should have known."

"You couldn't have known Jason. You were so happy, you two and I was blaming you for my father, for my upbringing, for everything. You were a male, to me you were behaving like my dad, I transferred it all onto you."

She looked him in the eye. "I'm sorry for what I did I really am but I just wanted us to be together, to be happy."

He had to smile. "Hell of a way to show it."

"I know, I wanted so much for us to be a normal family, for us to be there for Hank, for him not to be scared…" she shrugged, "so I resorted to violence. Didn't learn anything did I?"

He ran his fingers down her cheek. "I don't know. You've at least apologised. Has your father?"

She shivered. "He said sorry a lot but I don't think that counts. It's as if he can't stop himself, as if he doesn't even know he's doing something wrong."

"Maybe he doesn't, maybe that's what he was brought up with." He took her hand again and squeezed it gently. "I'm not making excuses though, I'm just saying…"

"Maybe he didn't know any better?"

"Maybe."

Cindy suddenly stood up, almost stumbling as she did. "Well fuck him! Whether he didn't know any better or not, he's a prick and when we get home I'm going to tell him that."

Jason laughed, "Maybe we should stop and buy a baseball bat on the way."

Cindy grimaced.

“Sorry,” he said, “that’s not that funny is it?”

Now she laughed. “It wasn’t that, I just trod in the pizza.”

Eighteen

They were having breakfast in another café in Armidale. Cindy wasn't really hungry but Jason wanted something to eat besides Weet-Bix and toast. He didn't say anything about the coffee so she figured it must have been okay this time. Cindy wondered if the waiter being in his 50s and obviously the proprietor had improved the taste. Cindy ordered a fruit compote, Jason ordered pancakes.

"Are they as good as your dad's?" she asked as he smothered them in maple syrup.

"Not bad but Frank's were a touch better."

"Sure you're not getting just a touch nostalgic?"

He chewed slowly, taking his time to answer. "Well, I've got to have something good to remember about the old bastard."

"It can't have all been bad can it?" she said, "Surely you remember other things that were good?"

"No I guess it wasn't. It's funny Frank mentioning the Sunday drives. I do remember them. We used to get in the car, me and Bradley in the back, mum and Frank in the front and he'd turn the radio up and just drive." He smiled. "I don't know if he ever had a planned route, I liked to think that he didn't, that it was just luck of the draw."

She picked at the fruit, not really hungry but wanting something that would come back up easily. "What do you think now?"

"Well, for a while there I figured he must have known where he was going but these days I'm not so sure."

Cindy laughed. "The evidence would seem to be against him wouldn't it?"

Jason stirred his coffee. "Yeah. We always found little towns though, markets, farms that sold fresh produce, playgrounds. If it was off the cuff he had a damn good radar."

Cindy nodded. "We had Sunday drives too but they were always regimented. Everything was done to a time, a schedule. We'd get ten minutes exactly in the playground, five minutes to eat our ice cream… we always knew where we were going too, there were no surprises."

Jason raised his cup for a refill. "But did you think like that then?"

She shook her head. "No, probably not."

Jason put his cup back down as the proprietor approached. "We had football too on a Saturday, that was always good." He waited for his cup to be refilled. "Of course at that age I didn't pay much attention to the actual games, we just ran around a lot."

Cindy grinned. "Us too. Dad liked his football. It was one of the few times we got a long leash. As long as we stayed close to the oval and reported back to him every quarter he'd let us go and play."

She shivered with the memory. "I loved Saturdays. Just playing with the other kids, digging around in the playground, running amok. I got my first kiss at the football."

"Not your last I'm sure."

She slapped him on the hand playfully. "And what do you mean by that?"

"Oh nothing, nothing."

"You're not insinuating that I was easy are you?"

He smirked. "Easy? Christ no, you're the hardest work I've ever had."

"Good. As long as I'm not losing my touch."

She turned to the proprietor as he hovered nearby. "Is there any fishing around here?"

"Fishing?" He stopped, put the empty plates he was holding on the next table. "Well, there are trout farms. You need a permit though. Is that the sort of thing you're after?"

"I was just wondering," she said as she picked at her compote.

"Well," he said as he recommenced cleaning up, "just out of town there are a couple of nice places. If you decide you want to give it a try I can get the numbers for you."

Cindy nodded. "Thanks."

Jason looked over at her. "Fishing? When did you get interested in fishing?"

"It was something we did as kids. Dad would take Malcolm fishing every now and then and I'd tag along sometimes." She pushed her plate aside. "I think I enjoyed it more than Malcolm actually. I loved skewering the worms on the hooks."

"That doesn't surprise me at all. Did you have any luck?"

She frowned in concentration. "You know, I really don't know. I used to catch a few but Dad always made me throw them back. I think he was upset that I would do better than my brother." She shrugged. "I guess I must have ruined his father/son bonding thing. I know he stopped taking me."

"Dave did take Brad and I fishing occasionally but we couldn't sit still long enough, well I couldn't. He soon gave up," Jason shrugged, "funnily enough though when I was 16/17 I used to go with Pete and Johnno and we had a ball. The booze probably helped."

Cindy smiled. "Catch anything?"

"Of course not. That would ruin the drinking."

Jason turned and signaled for the bill. "Guess we better get going then, unless you really did want to fish."

Cindy considered the idea for a moment. "Maybe it would be fun. I've never fished for trout."

Jason looked out at the skies. The clouds were looking ominous. "I don't think you're going to get the chance today either. Unless you fancy getting soaked doing it."

Cindy's brow creased. "No, I guess not. I can't say that I liked the fishing that much. I guess it was just the nostalgia talking."

"Admit it, you just wanted to fondle some worms again didn't you?"

She stood up. "I've got you for that. And anyway, you don't use worms for trout you idiot, you use lures."

Jason could feel himself getting tired; he was struggling to concentrate on the long stretch of grey in front of him. "Talk to me, Cindy, I need something to keep me awake.”

“Huh?” Cindy sat straight, having dozed off herself.

“Engage me in meaningless conversation or I’ll fall asleep and we’ll end up as just another set of statistics.”

“Oh, okay. What should I talk about?”

He looked at her, frowned. “Your choice but not Nancy. Just keep me alert.”

Cindy sat quietly for a moment. “Okay then, what’s the most embarrassing thing you’ve ever done?”

“Shit, I don’t know. I’ll have to think about that. Do blackouts count?”

“We’re you embarrassed by them?”

“Not really. Most of the time I have no idea what people are talking about.”

She moved across the seat to be next to him. “What do you mean?”

“I mean, when people tell me what I’ve done…I don’t remember most of it anyway.”

“Well, then, blackouts definitely don’t count.”

He liked the feel of her body pressed against him, her smell, her smoothness. He’d missed all that when they’d been apart. “What’s your most embarrassing moment?”

“Besides being your partner in public?”

“Very funny.”

“Okay…well, besides wearing those hospital gowns that never quite covered my big bum, I’d have to say it was when I threw up on my windscreen.”

“You did what?” he chuckled. “I thought vomiting was my territory.”

“It was during the chemo…it always made me nauseous. I was driving home from a check-up. Well, my friend Sam was driving but it was my car…and I burped and spewed all over the windscreen, all over the dash… took weeks to get the smell out.” She smirked. “Sam never volunteered to drive me again. In fact I didn’t see much of him at all after that.”

“I never liked him anyway.”

"You saw him once, Jason, and you were drunk." Her hand rested on his leg, tickling his inner thigh. "Your turn now."

"I'm still getting over the image of you chucking. At least if you'd done it on the outside you could have used the wipers."

Cindy slapped his leg. "C'mon stop delaying…most embarrassing moment now!"

He shrugged, could feel the colour rising to his cheeks already. "Okay then, here goes. Don't know what made me think of this, maybe it's your hand on my leg…"

"What does that mean?"

"Well, when I was about 10 or 11 I started getting serious boners…"

She poked him. "Late bloomer then?"

He ignored her. "And one day when I was in the bath, well, I was washing my dick and…" He paused. "You sure you want to hear this?"

"Oh yeah, don't stop now, I'm right on the cusp."

"Very funny." He was feeling slightly uncomfortable now and Cindy's hand was starting to inch up his thigh. "Anyway I was washing myself, nothing sinister or sexual. Hell, I was only a kid…"

"A well-developed one I'd say on the evidence before me." Cindy started to rub the front of his jeans.

"And I jacked myself off without even knowing it. Came in the bath."

"That's it? What's so embarrassing about that?" Cindy unzipped him. He was finding it difficult now to concentrate on the road or his story.

"When I got out of the bath I went and told Mum and Dave that something weird had happened. That I'd peed in the bath but it was kinda white and sticky."

Cindy stopped. "You did what?"

"I know, I know. Anyway, Mum and Dave looked at each other, then Dave took me aside, gave me the birds and bees lecture and I haven't left it alone since." He turned his head to her. "Be careful there, you're playing with a loaded gun."

"At least I know what I'm doing with it." He had to agree with her.

Nineteen

They were driving through the main street of Glen Innes when Jason saw them. "Hey, that's Col and Ralphy."

Cindy turned. "Who?"

He pointed to the footpath. "There, the big guy there." Jason swung the Holden into a parking space, honking his horn as he did. He saw Col looking around, a puzzled expression on his face. Jason unbuckled, jumped out of the car. "Col, Ralph, how are you?"

A smile crossed Col's face. "Jason, how are ya, lad?" They shook hands all round and Jason introduced them to Cindy.

"What's a fine girl like you doing with a bum like this?" asked Ralph, "Dump him and run away with me."

Cindy laughed. "You find gold, Ralph, and I just might."

"Fancy a beer then?" asked Col.

Jason hesitated. "I'm driving and we've still got a fair way to go."

Cindy took his arm. "It's okay, Jase, I'm sure one beer won't matter."

They walked into the bar, finding a corner table near the window. Cindy sat herself in the sunlight, feeling cold and weary already.

"You okay?" asked Jason.

She nodded. "Just tired. Can you get me a mineral water?"

After the drinks came, Jason turned his attention to Col and Ralphy. "So what are you guys doing up here? Given up prospecting?"

"No, nothing like that," said Ralph as he sipped his beer. "We're still looking for gold. We're just having a break…"

He looked at Col. "Yeah, a break."

Jason looked at their faces. "Is something going on?"

Col blushed. "We got into a bit of a fight back at the caravan park, the cops were called."

"So we thought we'd get out of town for a few days," continued Ralph, "let things cool down."

Col put down his now-empty glass. "And, you know, there are sapphires up this way, so we thought we'd give them a try. Another round?"

Again Jason hesitated.

"Aah…"

Cindy nudged him. "Go on, we're in no hurry."

Col got up and went to the bar.

"So what about this fight?" asked Cindy.

Ralph looked over at Col as he stood at the bar. "Boofhead there punched out some loudmouth. No big deal really, 'cept his brother's the local copper."

"Good idea to get out of town for a little while then."

"You don't know the half of it, young lady."

Col came back, glancing coldly at Ralph as he put the beers down. "I don't think we need to go there Ralphy."

"Sorry mate, wasn't thinking."

Jason tried not to sound nervous. "Something wrong Col?"

Col looked over the table at Cindy. "It's not something I'm proud of," he paused, "I've had a bit of domestic trouble in the past…"

"Domestic trouble?" asked Cindy quietly.

Col raised his hands defensively. "It's not what you think. I never hit Jeannie or the kids. I wouldn't do that."

He put his hands back down on the table, resting them palms down. "But I'm on probation you see… so I can't really afford any trouble."

"Col's not supposed to have crossed the border without telling someone," Ralphy added slowly.

"Probation?" Jason knew he sounded nervous now.

Col looked down at his mauled fingers. "I violated a restraining order. Wanted to see the kids was all… suspended sentence but I'm on good behaviour." He looked up at Cindy again. "I never hit them but you don't have to do you? I mean the damage ain't just physical is it?"

Ralph patted Col's shoulder. "It's alright mate."

Col shook his head. "No it's not alright Ralphy. You know don't you love? It's not alright."

Cindy nodded slowly unable to look away. There were tears in the big man's eyes and she realised with a start that her own cheeks were wet.

"We were young when we got married, Jeannie and me. And I thought I was doing the right thing, working hard, food in our bellies, roof over our heads… I won't deny that it was tough at times, with four kids, one income but we managed."

He wiped the tears from his eyes. "A man gets tired though, working all the time, another kid to feed, another bill to pay and things don't always go the way they should and there's only so much you can do…"

He curled his hand up into a fist. "But what sort of man would I be to use this on a kid? That ain't right. No matter how tired I was or how much pressure I was under."

He shook his head. "No, I never hit 'em but I hurt 'em anyway. You don't have to hit 'em to hurt 'em."

He picked up his beer, took a long drink and put the now half empty glass down. Jason was watching Cindy. She was still staring at Col, the tears damp on her cheeks.

"No you don't have to hit them," she said in a whisper.

Col nodded just slightly. "I'd yell at them, at Jeannie too. I'd come home from work and take it out on them, not physically you know but still yelling and screaming, bullying them almost. I never touched 'em though. But when I came home they'd scatter, afraid of what might happen."

Ralph coughed and pushed his chair back. "Come on Col, I think it might be time to go."

"No mate, I'm not finished." He pointed to his glass but they all knew that wasn't what he meant.

"I never touched them, not once. Not even when Jeannie took the kids and up and left me. I never ever hit them but it didn't matter did it? I thought I was doing okay but you know they hated me, they were afraid of me. I kept trying to patch things up, promising I'd get help, that it would all be okay but of course I'd just end up yelling, trying to bully her back into coming home. And then one day my eldest boy Mickey…" Col choked back a sob, his throat tightened, "Mickey, he… he… he stood up to me. Barely nine years old, skinny little Mickey and he said, 'dad, if you ever come near mum again I'll kill you.' He was trying to protect his mum from me… from his dad."

He picked up his glass, looked at it carefully. "Of course this stuff didn't help but that ain't any excuse. It was me not the booze or the job or my old man's discipline. There aren't any excuses for being what I was… except maybe ignorance." He put the glass down gently and looked at Cindy. "No excuses though."

Cindy reached over to his scarred hands, resting her fingers on top. "I won't tell you it's alright Col because it isn't. What you did wasn't good but at least you know that you were wrong, at least you can admit that," She took a deep breath, "and at least you didn't hit them, you have that on your side."

"I just want to be able to see my kids, to make up for what I put them through. If I can just say I'm sorry to them and maybe explain that I made mistakes." He hung his head. "I just want them to know I love them is all."

Ralph tapped the table with his glass. "I'd just like to share something here. Something this big galoot won't tell you. See that bloke he snotted at the caravan park…"

Jason interrupted, "The local cop's brother?"

"Yeah the cop's brother. Well he was a nasty piece of work. I'm not defending Col for what he did but this bloke did hit his kids. That's why Col decked him. It don't make up for anything I know but I just wanted you to know that's all."

Col shook his head. "It don't make up for anything Ralphy."

Ralph laughed. "I know mate but hell it bought a cheer from more than a few folk at the caravan park."

Jason couldn't help but smile. He looked at Cindy and she was smiling too.

Col shrugged. "Sorry to unload on you like that but when you've only got Ralphy here to talk to…"

Cindy nodded. "I know the feeling. I've only got this old man here."

"Good thing you have very little to say then isn't it?" laughed Jason. "Another drink?"

Col looked at Cindy. "As long as you don't mind drinking with me?"

"It's okay Col, I'll have a drink with you. But you have to promise me something."

"Anything I can do for you I will."

"When you do go home, you have to see someone about your temper, about your anger. Don't let your kids grow up only knowing fear."

Col lowered his head, he felt like a school boy again, being told what to do but he knew she was right. "I'll do that. For you I'll do that." He looked up again, his eyes watery. "Thank you."

Ralph sniffed, wiped his eyes. "Right, enough of that you two, one more beer then we got sapphires to find. Man's going to need money if he wants to get his life back on track."

By the time they left the pub, after staying for lunch and another couple of rounds, Jason was feeling quite a buzz. "I don't think I should drive."

"That's okay, let's hang around here for awhile." Cindy took his arm. "I want to stay with you, Jason, I don't want to go home."

He was feeling light-headed, dizzy. "What do you mean? Of course you're going home. That's why we're here." He sat on the bonnet of the car. "Besides, we're nearly there now."

"I know that but I don't want to go any more. I want to be with you." She sat next to him. "Can't we just turn around, go back?"

Jason shook his head slowly. "Cindy, your mum and dad are waiting for you. I said I'd take you home and that's what I'm going to do. I can understand you not wanting to see your dad, but your mum is waiting too." He didn't want to say it but he doubted whether she could make it back if they turned around now. He put his arm around her waist, pulled her closer. "But I guess a day or two won't matter. Let's check out the sights. We'll have to walk though, I'm not getting behind the wheel right now."

"Can't handle your booze huh?" she laughed.

He liked the sound, it made him feel even more light-headed. "I can handle anything you've got girl."

"Yeah? There might be a test later."

They started walking up the street. "Oh good, I've always been good at them."

She giggled, "Well if you fail I might just get out the cane."

"Now you're talking," he laughed until he got hiccups.

They wasted the afternoon looking at the historical sights and giggling like school kids.

They met up with Col and Ralph for tea that night. The boys had been fossicking.

"Had a bit of luck, too," said Col, "it's not what you know, it's who." He pulled out a dirty plastic bag. Half a dozen stones were visible. "Sapphire," he said, "not a bad afternoon's work."

"Really?" asked Cindy.

"Of course, they gotta be cut and polished," said Ralph, "but they're sapphires alright."

Col fished one out, dropped it into Cindy's palm. "For you young lady, something to say thank you and to remember us by."

Cindy turned red. "You didn't have to do that, Col. You boys worked hard for this."

"Hell, we'll find more."

"And if we don't," continued Ralph, "we'll come to Brisbane and get that one back."

"Yeah, may as well cross another state line," said Col as he put the other stones back into his jacket. "Now, we gonna eat? Being a fugitive from the law makes a man hungry."

Cindy was enjoying the company of these itinerant jokers. Despite their hardships, their injuries, their daily hand-to-mouth scramble for beer and food, despite all that they were having fun; they were taking what the world threw at them, catching it, molding it into their own shapes and throwing it back.

She laughed until her belly hurt that night, forgetting how drawn she felt, how little energy she had lately, how exhausting each day was becoming. When they finally left the pub and went back to their room she was too tired even to shoot up but it was a happy exhaustion, a joyful burning of the candle while there was still a flame to be seen.

She slept soundly, Jason watching over her, the news channel on in the corner for company.

In the morning they met Col and Ralphy for coffee before heading off.

"You look after this girl, Jason, or I'll be looking for you."

"Yeah, with his good eye too."

Jason smiled. "Don't worry, boys, I won't let her out of my sight."

"So what's next for you two?" asked Cindy.

"Few more days here till the heat's off, I reckon," said Ralphy, "then back to the gold mines."

"You still think there's gold there, then?"

"Oh it's there, don't worry about that, it's there."

"Well, I might just call in on the way back then."

"You do that, son, and bring Cindy with you. We could do with a woman's touch at that caravan park."

Jason blushed.

Cindy looked away. "I'm not coming back, Ralph, Queensland is the end of the line."

Ralph was quiet, embarrassed.

"Well," he finally said, "I guess that's our loss."

Cindy pecked them both lightly on the cheek. "Yes, I guess it is."

Twenty

The first time Cindy fell in love, she was 14. His name was Ronnie Watson and he was 17½. They fucked in the back of his dad's Cortina. She waited two weeks for him to call her.

She didn't get into the back of anyone's car again until she was 16. His name was 'Big' Ben Connolly. Big Ben was her first true love. He was a tanned, slick surf bum from the Gold Coast living off his father's investments. Cindy's parents hated him immediately.

That alone probably added an extra month to their 10-week relationship. Their days and nights were spent smoking, surfing and fucking, in that order.

Ben then gave her the crabs. She plucked them out, slowly, methodically and painfully, one by one, saved them in a medicine bottle and waited. They were at a party with all his mates; the big spring piss-up before they all went back to boarding school or uni or away with whichever parent currently had custody. It wasn't a maudlin affair, far from it, but there was still a sense of desperation in the air, of last-gasp words, final chances to say things, do deeds, make a name maybe for yourself.

They were all at an age where adulthood was breathing behind them, close and cold on the backs of their necks, fingers lightly tapping on shoulders, ruffling hair and whispering sweet nothing doings in their ears. An age where the spring piss-up could well be the last time you were all together on equal footing, still girls, still boys, still clutching at some vestige of childhood, of youthful exuberance, where you could still have fun and the consequences wouldn't bite back later on, to be found on your report, your record, your employment card.

It was at the spring piss-up that Cindy poured the lice into Ben's beer. She considered herself lucky to have escaped with minor facial bruising and a sprained wrist.

Now, as she sat in the car watching Jason cleaning the windscreen, she wondered what had happened to Ronnie and Ben and Sam and all the others.

Would any of them have done all this, taken care of her, fed her, held her, tolerated her?

She looked again at Jason. He wasn't the best looking guy she'd ever been with, hair too long, nose a touch too wide, but he had eyes a colour of which she'd never seen; a greenish grey sea of their own, clouded waters and unknown depths. Those eyes and a smile that could melt any girl's heart (even her mother had fallen for it) were more than enough to make up for his shortcomings.

As he worked so diligently now on such a simple task, his features set so seriously, she wished it could again be like it was when they first got together. When that smile had first caught her attention, when those eyes had first watched her as she ran around the bar, reveling in the noise and the music and the fun she was having. It wasn't until much later that she realised that it seemed that everything they did together those first few months was accompanied by noise. There was always sound, music, a cacophony of voices, engines, stereos, cars, people, life. They rarely slept. Instead they would sit in her room, ignoring her housemates, stereo turned up, drinking, smoking, fucking, talking. When the others weren't around they would move into her backyard or the kitchen and continue. Talking, making coffee or mixing bourbon and cokes, fucking as the want took either of them, making toast or two-minute noodles; the radio or tape deck always turned up loud to accompany them through their day. More than once they'd been spotted naked, rutting in her backyard by the brewery drivers as their trucks rumbled past her back fence to drop off deliveries to the hotel next door. In fact the hotel, the service station across the road, the main thoroughfare that ran so close to her home all added industrial noise, motion, human traffic to the mood of their days and nights. She didn't really think of herself as a social person, far from it really but the people, the energy, the music and constant chatter, the noises and movement, the chaos and comings and goings were food to her. She felt like a vampire at times, feeding not on blood but the action and sounds, the frivolity and gossip, movement, noise, dancing, fighting. It was all there for her to soak in, soak up and Jason was there for a time too, sitting with her or standing beside her as she laughed and joked and pulled strings, manipulating people and sneering at their banality, their inane desire to be wanted or noticed or needed. She always thought she was better than them, superior maybe that she needed no one but herself to survive. She was wrong of course, she needed the noise, she needed the music, the motion and action, it was what kept her sane. She realised now it kept her from remembering too. Much later she would realise that she needed Jason as well. He'd played along then with her stunts, her childish pranks, her need for attention. Maybe not completely comfortable with it but he'd never stopped her, never censured her. When she dropped a cockroach in his beer he calmly fished it out and offered to give it mouth-to-mouth. He then helped arrange the funeral pyre in the ashtray. When she started dropping cockroaches in other people's beer, he'd buy them another. He laughed when she set fire to Jimmy the Weed's hair, telling him he should wash it more often, helped hand out toilet paper to people on the street, even got in a fistfight one night when someone objected to the earthworms writhing in their ashtray. He lost the fight but she fucked him as a thank-you anyway.

His eyes were still that colour, that unknown sea of grey, green light but there were bags under them now. His hair was pulled back into a ponytail, lank and greasy. He looked a lot like she felt. But that smile was still there, if and when he cared to unleash it. She was going to miss that smile.

They were passing a hire car with Queensland plates. Cindy nodded at the car and said, "Sam told me once that the hire cars in Queensland have their brakes adjusted to pull to the left or at least the ones on the Gold Coast do." Jason glanced at her. "Yeah? Why?" he asked skeptically.

"All the American tourists. Whenever they got themselves in to trouble they'd veer to the right on instinct. You know because they're used to driving on the right and all."

He looked at her. "Bullshit."

"No," she shook her head, "Sam said they would adjust the brakes to pull to the left to compensate for the Americans."

"And how did the mighty Sam know all this?"

She smiled. "He was a chef in one of the hotels and someone told him about it."

"A chef huh?" He glanced in the mirror at the now disappearing car. "Probably really worked at McDonalds."

"Steady now, that's not jealousy I hear is it?" She poked him in the arm.

"Jealous? Me? Of that git, fat chance."

"Jason, you met him once, you were drunk and he was a very nice bloke."

"He didn't last though did he?" he said with some venom in his voice.

She frowned. "What do you want, a blow by blow description of our relationship?"

He turned to her, "No, just the bits that went wrong. It'll make me feel a little less inadequate."

Cindy laughed, "Sorry lover but in this case you were inadequate."

"Thanks, that's really made me like him more."

She ran a hand up his arm. "Look it doesn't matter, he's gone and you're here." She punched him playfully. "Who knows maybe he's shacked up with Lindsay or Nancy or even Amy by now. It is a small town after all."

"Hopefully not that small." He overtook another hire car. "So if he was so good why didn't he stay up on the Gold Coast?"

"Wanderlust," she waved a hand in the air, "he just couldn't stay in one place."

Jason cocked an eyebrow. "Wanderlust?"

"Okay, maybe the food poisoning scare had something to do with it too."

"And he ended up cooking at the Duke?"

She grinned. "Yeah."

Jason shook his head, "You find them don't you?"

"He seemed like a nice guy Jason, it was a very nice change. He was so straight and normal compared to everyone else I'd been seeing."

"I think I've just been insulted but then again…"

"You know he listened to Bon Jovi when we were in bed together."

"Well," he said, taking his hands off the wheel, "that explains it all. No wonder you fell for him."

"Just drive the car smart arse."

She stretched her legs and slumped back in the seat. "Anyway, he was a nice guy, he just didn't last that's all." She thought about Sam, about his big double bed, the radio always on some commercial station, the leftovers in the fridge, the wide screen TV. He was so straight, so centred on work and owning things and being seen as a good, normal guy. He was so different to Jason and yet for a while she had really liked him, or so she thought. Even the Bon Jovi had grown on her after a while though she wasn't about to admit that to Jason. She wasn't sure what had gone wrong really. No, that wasn't true. She knew what it was really, it was Sam's insistence that she modify her behaviour, that she slow down and act like a responsible adult, like his girlfriend should act. She had already toned down her wildness anyway, or so she thought but he still wanted her to be more like the women on those stupid shows he always watched on TV, like the dutiful wife and girlfriend, he didn't want the high-spirited girl she really was, he wanted a watered down and palatable version of her. Cindy wasn't prepared to do that, she didn't think she really could ever be that watered down anyway, whether Bon Jovi had grown on her or not. Who knows, she thought wryly, maybe he did end up with Nancy. She did seem more like his sort of girl. She was delighted within herself for just a moment that the old bitchy Cindy still had some spark in her. Jason noticed an evil smirk flicker across her face but said nothing. Whatever she was thinking about right now, he didn't want to know.

Another hire car was coming up in front of them. "What is this? Is there a bloody convention on or something?"

Cindy glanced at the car as they passed. "Don't know. Maybe school holidays?"

"No, you don't need a hire car for that just patience."

They pulled back into their own lane. "Do you ever wonder what we'd be doing now if he hadn't died?"

"Of course I do," she said slowly, "I think of him all the time."

Jason smiled, "I sometimes wonder what he'd be like now, what sort of trouble he'd be giving us…"

"How he'd go at school?" she interrupted him, "what his friends would be like?"

"Yeah," he nodded, "all that sort of stuff."

"This could have been a holiday trip for us couldn't it?" she said as she gazed out the window.

He glanced at her, saw the tears reflected in the window. "Don't cry girl, I can't stand a crying girl, makes me go all soft."

She turned, wiped her cheek. "You always were soft anyway you wimp. Hank had you around his little finger."

"He did not." He pointed to his chest. "Why I can remember at least once when I told him off."

"Oh yeah, I remember that." She giggled. "He touched your Dead Boys album and you nearly ran across the room to get it off of him."

"Oh yeah, that time too. I was thinking of the time he found your vibrator under the bed."

Cindy went red. "You didn't tell him off, you brought him into the lounge with it to show my parents."

He shrugged. "Well, I told him off before I brought it in. I distinctly remember saying to him, 'naughty boy let's go and find mum and she can put it away.'"

"Well you're lucky I didn't put it away right then and there, up your arse."

Jason rolled his eyes. "You've tried worse things."

Cindy flicked open the glove box. "Do you think it's time for Hi-5 yet?"

"Why not? It ain't Bon Jovi I know but Charlie is cuter."

When Jason started crying in the main street of Casino, tears streaming down his face as he struggled to control his emotions, his hand clutching a burnt sausage in a piece of bread, onion rings balancing precariously on top amidst the sauce, that was when Cindy realised just how hard this journey was for him.

It was Beef Week in Casino and barbecues dotted the street. Now, as Jason cried, a young apprentice, hairnet on, red shirt untucked and stained with offal and margarine, stood quietly wondering what he'd done wrong and whether he was going to get in trouble for it. He shuffled back a step or two and decided to concentrate on turning the sausages, hoping the old guy and his girlfriend would move on before his boss came out to see what was happening.

Cindy took Jason gently by the arm and steered him towards a bench. "What happened then? The sausages aren't that bad, are they?"

He tried to smile, gave up and, shaking his head, started bawling. People stopped, looking at this couple, obviously out-of-towners, druggies from the coast most probably, then walked on, tut-tutting.

Cindy was oblivious to their stares, she just rubbed his back and arms, reciting over and over, "its okay, Jase, its okay."

Finally, he stopped, wiped his eyes, sniffed and looked at the now-cold sausage on the bench next to him. "Guess I'll need another one."

Cindy smiled. "I'd better get it." The apprentice was hesitant when she came back over. "No onions this time," she joked, "they make him cry."

"Is he okay?" He nodded his head towards Jason who sat looking at his hands.

"Yeah, it's been a long week, that's all. He's just tired."

The boy nodded, pretending to understand, though he didn't really. You want a long week, he thought, try manning a barbecue every day for a guy who won't pay overtime and who still won't tell me if I've got a full-time job. He handed over the sausage, a splash of home-brand sauce smothering the burnt section and retreated back to tend the onions.

Cindy handed Jason the food. "So what happened?"

He took a bite, chewing slowly. "The monster fete."

"The what?" She stared into his eyes. What was he talking about?

"The monster fete. Remember? We took Hank." He gestured with the burnt offering. "The church hall…lucky dips…sausage sizzle…" He could feel a fresh tear trickling down his cheek. "And Hank said…"

Cindy suddenly remembered. In unison they said it, "But where are the monsters, Daddy?"

They smiled at each other, and then Cindy started giggling. "He was so disappointed, wasn't he?"

"Wasn't he just?" Jason found himself giggling too then laughing out loud at the memory of Hank looking so earnestly between the crochet dolls and second-hand books for the monster stall. Finally, triumphantly, he'd found a Hungry Jacks giveaway for 50 cents, something from *Monsters Inc.*

"Look, Daddy, Mummy, its Mike. This really is a monster fete."

The apprentice watched them both as they started laughing till tears ran down their cheeks. He decided it was time to shut the barbecue.

Hell, he didn't like meat anyway. Some days he felt sick just from the sight of the stuff let alone the smell. Maybe working as a pump jockey for Uncle Phil wasn't such a bad option after all. He turned off the jets and started packing up the barbecue tools as Jason and Cindy got up, still smiling and walked back to the car, both wondering what had happened to Mike.

Jason nodded as they walked past. "Nice sausages mate."

The boy nodded back. Maybe a job where you didn't deal with the public at all would be better. He wondered if it was too late to re-enroll for Year 11.

Twenty One

It was like a bad dream. Jason blinked and then blinked again, then he pinched his cheek. It was still there.

Should he wake Cindy? He looked at her, mouth open, eyes closed, so relaxed against the doorframe. He turned his attention back to the apparition in front of him.

Rising above the highway, the fields, poking out of the early morning mist was a prawn, a giant prawn. Jason wondered if his beer had been spiked last night. Was this thing real or was he, in fact, asleep as well?

He pinched his cheek again, feeling the stab of pain – no, he was definitely awake. He started to panic, too tired to think rationally. Was this how it would all end? So close to the last stop, within a day's drive of their final destination. Crushed by some freak of fucking nature in a coastal town he'd never heard of, a wrong turn bringing them here in the first place. Where the hell was Ballina anyway?

He could feel the sweat beading on his temple as this thing drew nearer. No, he realised, it wasn't moving towards them, they were moving towards it. The car, of course.

He brought his foot down hard on the brakes, the tires squealed in resentment, he could smell rubber burning, the car bucking in protest but he held firm.

"Fuck you, you steroid-abusing crayfish, you ain't getting me!"

Cindy was jolted awake. She tried to make some sense of the moment. The car was skidding sideways down the road, Jason was wide-eyed, swearing, screaming. She shook her head, trying to clear the dreams. The car suddenly stopped.

She could smell the rubber, it made her nauseous but she dare not move. Jason was still raving, something about nature's revenge, giant crabs, crustacean armies and Guy N. Smith.

He kept pointing out of his side window, shaking his fist. Slowly, she inched her way across the bench seat towards him. Sweat was running down his face despite the cold, his eyes still wide, were red and bloodshot. He looked so tired, so shattered and drawn, for a moment it felt to her like she was the healthy one and he was dying.

"Jason, Jason," she called softly, 'what's going on?"

Her turned to her too quickly and she had to jump back to avoid their heads colliding. "It's alright Cindy. I stopped just in time. The fucker won't get us now."

He was pointing out of the window again. There was a sea mist slowly dissolving but still making vision hazy, like looking through gauze bandage.

She squinted and tried to take in the shapes, the movement. With a jolt she saw it and burst out laughing.

Jason was stunned. "What's so fucking funny? It could have killed us."

"It's the Big Prawn, you idiot. Like the Big Orange, the Giant Koala…it's not real, it's a tourist trap."

He looked at her, looked back out the window, looked back at her. It was silent now, Cindy not sure whether to laugh or run. The engine had cut out when Jason slammed the brakes on and he could still hear it ticking as it cooled down.

"It's not real?"

"Of course it's not." She took his hand in hers. "I think maybe we should take a break."

Jason nodded, still not convinced that monster out there in the fog was fibreglass and wire, that it wasn't real and waiting for them to climb out the car.

"Yeah, sure…I'm feeling very tired actually, very tired."

They drove carefully down to the beach. The mist slowly lifted to reveal the waves rolling in, colliding with the shore before retreating and trying again.

A few surfers were out braving the cool morning. Jason laid his head on Cindy's shoulder and they watched the waves coming in, going out, coming in, going out…

They fell asleep, Jason first, then Cindy.

When Cindy woke up, Jason was sitting on the bonnet of the car, his back to her. She climbed out of the Holden, stretched her arms high and felt the breeze tickle her now-bare midriff.

She walked around to the front of the car. Jason looked up, he was smiling.

In his hand were photos; photos of her and of Hank. "You scrub up alright, you know."

She climbed up next to him, feeling the warmth coming off the car and spreading down her legs. "Let me see those damn things."

He handed the photos over. It was Hank's birthday party. A cake in the shape of a four, party hats, Jason holding Hank up in the air, Hank's mouth open wide in delight. And there she was, hair washed, shining, cheeks full of colour, a proud mother with her family. It felt so strange now; it was like it was someone else in that photo – another Cindy, another lifetime.

Surely that smiling girl, bouncing, full of vim, so proud of herself was not the same person, not the girl who got thrown out of school, who caused so much pain to her mum, who fucked up everything she touched, who was no good for nothing, at least according to her father, surely that girl wasn't her.

The next photo was Hank holding a piece of his cake, icing smeared across his mouth and chin, grinning at the camera, paper hat perched on his head, toy car in his other hand.

In the background she could make out her own shape, round and full, oozing life and vitality; it was like looking at ghosts.

She handed the photos back. "I don't think I can look at them anymore."

Jason nodded. "I know. It's hard at first but I like to remind myself of the fun, the good stuff…I like to remember when we were a family. I can't get it back but at least I can remember it."

He picked out a photo. It was all three of them, smiling happily but not posed, not cheesy. There was a genuine joy in their faces, their stance that showed, even in flat gloss no borders.

Of course, Hank was on a sugar high and Jason had one or two bourbons under his belt at that stage but there was no denying the happiness their faces showed, the glee with which Hank clung to Cindy, toy car still clutched in his mitt. He passed the photo to Cindy.

"I know it makes you sad but it should make you happy. These were great days."

She took the photo, tears running down her cheeks and looked back at her best days.

"I know Jason, I know." She kissed him on the cheek. "Thank you…for Hank…for us…for this…"

He pulled out another photo. Her mother standing proudly beside Cindy, Jason and Hank. "She's a strong one your mum, now I understand where you get it."

Cindy sniffed. "Yeah she is. I guess I have to go home to see her at least. I owe her that much."

"I'm glad you feel that way," he smiled, "because it's a long way back."

She handed him back the photo. "But you'd take me back if I asked, wouldn't you?"

"Yeah," he said, "I probably would."

She touched his cheek gently, smelling just a breeze of Old Spice on her fingers. "I don't think I've ever told you Jason Myers but I love you."

He looked at her face, seeing again that smile, that girl that had first caught his eye. He felt something inside him, like a surge of power, it hurt his chest so much that he wanted to scream but then it felt good too. "You know, I think I've loved you since the first moment I saw you."

She punched his arm. "You old romantic you. How could any girl resist?"

They lie back on the bonnet and let the morning sun warm them. Neither of them said anything, they just held hands and let the tears slide down their cheeks.

They decided to book a room at a motel and stay overnight.

Jason pulled the photo album out of the bottom of his bag, meant as a present for Cindy's parents, and they spent the afternoon and the evening alternating between tears and laughter as they looked back over their life together, neither saying anything about what tomorrow might bring.

In the morning Jason felt better, refreshed and woke up laughing as he recalled the giant prawn and his panic attack. He turned to Cindy's side of the bed but it was empty.

Without thinking he got out of bed and walked into the bathroom. Cindy sat fully clothed on the toilet seat, her sleeve rolled up, a needle in her hand. Her arm was a dark blue/red, pus oozed from the needle marks in her elbow and forearm.

"I think I've got an infection," she deadpanned.

"Christ. You need a doctor."

"Why? I've only got a couple of hundred k's to go, Jason. I'm nearly home."

He wanted to slap her but stopped himself. "I can't take you home like this."

"Don't worry, Dad will blame me, not you."

"I don't care what they think, I can't let you go like this." He helped her to stand. "We've got to find you a doctor, you need something for that."

"No." She sat back down, grimacing as she banged her arm on the way. "It doesn't matter now, don't you see? I'm ready. I want to be with Hank. Just get me home, I want to die at home." The tears ran freely down her cheeks, salt stinging as they splashed on her arm. "Just get me home."

There were to be no more stops, except for petrol. It was straight through to Redland Bay. No piss breaks, no smack, no coffee, just bitumen rolling under the car as they headed home.

Cindy curled up on the bench seat, her head resting on Jason's lap. On the tape deck was AC/DC's *Highway To Hell*: '…no stop signs, speed limits, nobody's gonna slow me down…' He cried for the first 75 kilometres.

Cindy died less than a block from home. She was dreaming of Hank. It was his first day of school. As he came running to her he held a painting, bright yellow and blue with 'Mum' written in the corner.

"It's an angel," he said. A small smile creased her mouth. She stopped breathing.

Epilogue

Jason sat nervously in the coffee shop. It was hot up here but crisp, clean, very little humidity. Darwin in the dry season was beautiful he'd once been told and so far he couldn't really argue with that assessment.

He was waiting for Cassie and her mother. He wanted to meet his half-sister, to see who she was, how she was. He wanted her to know she had another family out there, down south in the cold. He wanted to tell her about Bradley and Rachel, about the new baby; he wanted her to know about Cindy, about Hank, about the lives they had led. He wanted her to know that she was not alone, that she was a member of a much bigger clan and that they would always be there for her. He stared out the window watching everyone as they walked by, wondering if he would recognize his half-sister when she did arrive.

The heat made his arm itch and he scratched at his new tattoo. Cindy looked at him, eyes brighter than they'd been in a long time. He smiled. "She'll be here soon, Cindy. Hope she doesn't look too much like me, poor kid."

The waitress at the counter watched him talking to himself but said nothing. This was Darwin, nothing surprised her anymore.

When Cassie walked in the door, Jason recognised her straightaway. It was the eyes, green grey seas you could drown in. He got up and walked towards her.

Winner of the Poetry Unleashed Festival 2010 Single Poet Collection Award, Kami's work can be found in publications and journals both nationally and internationally, as well as on the odd toilet wall. His novellas, S.F.&T. and Bunk Beds & Chilli Vodka were published by Paroxysm Press and the main characters from Fists Of Love were first found in S.F.& T.

He has performed in Adelaide, Melbourne, Sydney and Newcastle including the Adelaide Fringe Festival, the National Young Writers Festival and the Melbourne Writers Festival. In 2009 and 2011 he represented South Australia at the Australian Poetry Slam national final in Sydney. As a spoken word performer, he has supported national and international musical acts in Adelaide and Sydney. Kami has organised and hosted slams, book launches and readings, as well as chairing and appearing on writing panels both in SA and interstate. In 2021 he was a recipient of the Writers SA Writers and Readers in Residency Program, and was Writer In Residence at Meningie Area School and Millicent High School as part of the Writers SA 2023 program.